THE UNIVERSE WAS FIVE MILES LONG . . .

and 2000 feet across. Men scoffed at the legends of such things as stars, or the demented idea that the Ship was moving . . . for the Ship *was* the Universe, and there could be nothing outside. Then one man found his way to a forgotten room, and saw the stars—and they moved. . . .

ORPHANS OF THE SKY, exciting in its plot and action, and stimulating in its speculation, is a science fiction landmark.

ROBERT A. HEINLEIN

Orphans of the Sky

A BERKLEY MEDALLION BOOK
PUBLISHED BY
BERKLEY PUBLISHING CORPORATION

Published by arrangement with G. P. Putnam's Sons

SBN 425-04410-6

BERKLEY MEDALLION BOOKS *are published by*
Berkley Publishing Corporation
200 Madison Avenue
New York, N.Y. 10016

BERKLEY MEDALLION BOOKS ® TM 757,375

Printed in the United States of America

BERKLEY MEDALLION EDITION,
NOVEMBER. 1970
THIRTEENTH PRINTING

CONTENTS

Part One

UNIVERSE

I

UNIVERSE

The Proxima Centauri Expedition, sponsored by the Jordan Foundation in 2119, was the first recorded attempt to reach the nearer stars of this galaxy. Whatever its unhappy fate we can only conjecture. . . .
—Quoted from *The Romance of Modern Astrography,* by Franklin Buck, published by Lux Transcriptions, Ltd., 3.50 cr.

"THERE'S A MUTIE! Look out!"

At the shouted warning, Hugh Hoyland ducked, with nothing to spare. An egg-sized iron missile clanged against the bulkhead just above his scalp with force that promised a fractured skull. The speed with which he crouched had lifted his feet from the floor plates. Before his body could settle slowly to the deck, he planted his feet against the bulkhead behind him and shoved. He went shooting down the passageway in a long, flat dive, his knife drawn and ready.

He twisted in the air, checked himself with his feet against the opposite bulkhead at the turn in the passage from which the mutie had attacked him, and floated lightly to his feet. The other branch of the passage was empty. His two companions joined him, sliding awkwardly across the floor plates.

"Is it gone?" demanded Alan Mahoney.

"Yes," agreed Hoyland. "I caught a glimpse of it as

it ducked down that hatch. A female, I think. Looked like it had four legs."

"Two legs or four, we'll never catch it now," commented the third man.

"Who the Huff wants to catch it?" protested Mahoney. "*I* don't."

"Well, I do, for one," said Hoyland. "By Jordan, if its aim had been two inches better, I'd be ready for the Converter."

"Can't either one of you two speak three words without swearing?" the third man disapproved. "What if the Captain could hear you?" He touched his forehead reverently as he mentioned the Captain.

"Oh, for Jordan's sake," snapped Hoyland, "don't be so stuffy, Mort Tyler. You're not a scientist yet. I reckon I'm as devout as you are—there's no grave sin in occasionally giving vent to your feelings. Even the scientists do it. I've heard 'em."

Tyler opened his mouth as if to expostulate, then apparently thought better of it.

Mahoney touched Hoyland on the arm. "Look, Hugh," he pleaded, "let's get out of here. We've never been this high before. I'm jumpy—I want to get back down to where I can feel some weight on my feet."

Hoyland looked longingly toward the hatch through which his assailant had disappeared while his hand rested on the grip of his knife, then he turned to Mahoney. "O.K., kid," he agreed, "it's a long trip down anyhow."

He turned and slithered back toward the hatch, whereby they had reached the level where they now were, the other two following him. Disregarding the ladder by which they had mounted, he stepped off into the opening and floated slowly down to the deck fifteen feet below, Tyler and Mahoney close behind him. Another hatch, staggered a few feet from the first, gave access to a still lower deck. Down, down, down, and still farther down they dropped, tens and dozens of decks, each silent, dimly lighted, mysterious. Each time they fell a little faster, landed a little harder. Mahoney protested at last.

"Let's walk the rest of the way, Hugh. That last jump hurt my feet."

"All right. But it will take longer. How far have we got to go? Anybody keep count?"

"We've got about seventy decks to go to reach farm country," answered Tyler.

"How do you know?" demanded Mahoney suspiciously.

"I counted them, stupid. And as we came down I took one away for each deck."

"You did not. Nobody but a scientist can do numbering like that. Just because you're learning to read and write you think you know everything."

Hoyland cut in before it could develop into a quarrel. "Shut up, Alan. Maybe he can do it. He's clever about such things. Anyhow, it feels like about seventy decks—I'm heavy enough."

"Maybe he'd like to count the blades on my knife."

"Stow it, I said. Dueling is forbidden outside the village. That is the Rule." They proceeded in silence, running lightly down the stairways until increasing weight on each succeeding level forced them to a more pedestrian pace. Presently they broke through into a level that was quite brilliantly lighted and more than twice as deep between decks as the ones above it. The air was moist and warm; vegetation obscured the view.

"Well, down at last," said Hugh. "I don't recognize this farm; we must have come down by a different line than we went up."

"There's a farmer," said Tyler. He put his little fingers to his lips and whistled, then called, "Hey! Shipmate! Where are we?"

The peasant looked them over slowly, then directed them in reluctant monosyllables to the main passageway which would lead them back to their own village.

A brisk walk of a mile and a half down a wide tunnel moderately crowded with traffic—travelers, porters, an occasional pushcart, a dignified scientist swinging in a litter borne by four husky orderlies and preceded by his master-at-arms to clear the common crew out of the way—a mile and a half of this brought them to the common of their own village, a spacious compartment three decks high and perhaps ten times as wide. They split up and went their own ways, Hugh to his quarters in the barracks of the cadets—young bachelors who did not live with their parents. He washed himself, and went thence to the compartments of his uncle, for whom he worked for his meals. His aunt glanced up as he came in, but said nothing, as became a woman.

His uncle said, "Hello, Hugh. Been exploring again?"

"Good eating, Uncle. Yes."

His uncle, a stolid, sensible man, looked tolerantly amused. "Where did you go and what did you find?"

Hugh's aunt had slipped silently out of the compartment, and now returned with his supper which she placed before him. He fell to—it did not occur to him to thank her. He munched a bite before replying.

"Up. We climbed almost to the level-of-no-weight. A mutie tried to crack my skull."

His uncle chuckled. "You'll find your death in those passageways, lad. Better you should pay more attention to my business against the day when I'll die and get out of your way."

Hugh looked stubborn. "Don't you have any curiosity, Uncle?"

"Me? Oh, I was prying enough when I was a lad. I followed the main passage all the way around and back to the village. Right through the Dark Sector I went, with muties tagging my heels. See that scar?"

Hugh glanced at it perfunctorily. He had seen it many times before and heard the story repeated to boredom. Once around the Ship—*pfui!* He wanted to go everywhere, see everything, and find out the why of things. Those upper levels now—if men were not intended to climb that high, why had Jordan created them?

But he kept his own counsel and went on with his meal. His uncle changed the subject. "I've occasion to visit the Witness. John Black claims I owe him three swine. Want to come along?"

"Why, no, I guess not—Wait—I believe I will."

"Hurry up, then."

They stopped at the cadets' barracks, Hugh claiming an errand. The Witness lived in a small, smelly compartment directly across the Common from the barracks, where he would be readily accessible to any who had need of his talents. They found him sitting in his doorway, picking his teeth with a fingernail. His apprentice, a pimply-faced adolescent with an intent nearsighted expression, squatted behind him.

"Good eating," said Hugh's uncle.

"Good eating to you, Edard Hoyland. D'you come on business, or to keep an old man company?"

"Both," Hugh's uncle returned diplomatically, then explained his errand.

"So?" said the Witness. "Well—the contract's clear enough:

"Black John delivered ten bushels of oats,
Expecting his pay in a pair of shoats;
Ed brought his sow to breed for pig;
John gets his pay when the pigs grow big.

"How big are the pigs now, Edard Hoyland?"

"Big enough," acknowledged Hugh's uncle, "but Black claims three instead of two."

"Tell him to go soak his head. 'The Witness has spoken.'"

He laughed in a thin, high cackle.

The two gossiped for a few minutes, Edard Hoyland digging into his recent experiences to satisfy the old man's insatiable liking for details. Hugh kept decently silent while the older men talked. But when his uncle turned to go he spoke up. "I'll stay awhile, Uncle."

"Eh? Suit yourself. Good eating, Witness."

"Good eating, Edard Hoyland."

"I've brought you a present, Witness," said Hugh, when his uncle had passed out of hearing.

"Let me see it."

Hugh produced a package of tobacco which he had picked up from his locker at the barracks. The Witness accepted it without acknowledgment, then tossed it to his apprentice, who took charge of it.

"Come inside," invited the Witness, then directed his speech to his apprentice. "Here, you—fetch the cadet a chair."

"Now, lad," he added as they sat themselves down, "tell me what you have been doing with yourself."

Hugh told him, and was required to repeat in detail

all the incidents of his more recent explorations, the Witness complaining the meanwhile over his inability to remember exactly everything he saw.

"You youngsters have no capacity," he pronounced. "No capacity. Even that lout"——he jerked his head toward the apprentice——"he has none, though he's a dozen times better than you. Would you believe it, he can't soak up a thousand lines a day, yet he expects to sit in my seat when I am gone. Why, when I was apprenticed, I used to sing myself to sleep on a mere thousand lines. Leaky vessels——that's what you are."

Hugh did not dispute the charge, but waited for the old man to go on, which he did in his own time.

"You had a question to put to me, lad?"

"In a way, Witness."

"Well——out with it. Don't chew your tongue."

"Did you ever climb all the way up to no-weight?"

"Me? Of course not. I was a Witness, learning my calling. I had the lines of all the Witnesses before me to learn, and no time for boyish amusements."

"I had hoped you could tell me what I would find there."

"Well, now, that's another matter. I've never climbed, but I hold the memories of more climbers than you will ever see. I'm an old man. I knew your father's father, and his grandsire before that. What is it you want to know?"

"Well——" What was it he wanted to know? How could he ask a question that was no more than a gnawing ache in his breast? Still——"What is it all for, Witness? Why are there all those levels above us?"

"Eh? How's that? Jordan's name, son——I'm a Witness, not a scientist."

"Well——I thought you must know. I'm sorry."

"But I do know. What you want is the Lines from the Beginning."

"I've heard them."

"Hear them again. All your answers are in there, if you've the wisdom to see them. Attend me. No——this is a chance for my apprentice to show off his learning. Here, you! The Lines from the Beginning——and mind your rhythm."

The apprentice wet his lips with his tongue and began:

"In the Beginning there was Jordan, thinking His lonely
thoughts alone.

In the Beginning there was darkness, formless, dead, and
Man unknown.

Out of the loneness came a longing, out of the longing came
a vision,

Out of the dream there came a planning, out of the plan
there came decision—

Jordan's hand was lifted and the Ship was born!

Mile after mile of snug compartments, tank by tank for
the golden corn,

Ladder and passage, door and locker, fit for the needs of
the yet unborn.

He looked on His work and found it pleasing, meet for
a race that was yet to be.

He thought of Man—Man came into being—checked his
thought and searched for the key.

Man untamed would shame his Maker, Man unruled would
spoil the Plan;

So Jordan made the Regulations, orders to each single
man,

Each to a task and each to a station, serving a purpose
beyond their ken,

Some to speak and some to listen—order came to the ranks
of men.

Crew He created to work at their stations, scientists to
guide the Plan.

Over them all He created the Captain, made him judge of
the race of Man.

Thus it was in the Golden Age!

Jordan is perfect, all below him lack perfection in their
deeds.

Envy, Greed, and Pride of Spirit sought for minds to lodge
their seeds.

One there was who gave them lodging—accursed Huff,
the first to sin!

His evil counsel stirred rebellion, planted doubt where it
had not been;

Blood of martyrs stained the floor plates, Jordan's Captain
made the Trip.

Darkness swallowed up—"

The old man gave the boy the back of his hand, sharp across the mouth. "Try again!"

"From the beginning?"

"No! From where you missed."

The boy hesitated, then caught his stride:

"Darkness swallowed ways of virtue, Sin prevailed throughout the Ship . . ."

The boy's voice droned on, stanza after stanza, reciting at great length but with little sharpness of detail the old, old story of sin, rebellion, and the time of darkness. How wisdom prevailed at last and the bodies of the rebel leaders were fed to the Converter. How some of the rebels escaped making the Trip and lived to father the muties. How a new Captain was chosen, after prayer and sacrifice.

Hugh stirred uneasily, shuffling his feet. No doubt the answers to his questions were there, since these were the Sacred Lines, but he had not the wit to understand them. Why? What was it all about? Was there really nothing more to life than eating and sleeping and finally the long Trip? Didn't Jordan intend for him to understand? Then why this ache in his breast? This hunger that persisted in spite of good eating?

While he was breaking his fast after sleep an orderly came to the door of his uncle's compartments. "The scientist requires the presence of Hugh Hoyland," he recited glibly.

Hugh knew that the scientist referred to was Lieutenant Nelson, in charge of the spiritual and physical welfare of the Ship's sector which included Hugh's native village. He bolted the last of his breakfast and hurried after the messenger.

"Cadet Hoyland!" he was announced. The scientist looked up from his own meal and said:

"Oh, yes. Come in, my boy. Sit down. Have you eaten?"

Hugh acknowledged that he had, but his eyes rested with interest on the fancy fruit in front of his superior. Nelson followed his glance. "Try some of these figs. They're a new mutation---I had them brought all the way from the far side. Go ahead---a man your age always has somewhere to stow a few more bites."

Hugh accepted with much self-consciousness. Never before had he eaten in the presence of a scientist. The elder leaned back in his chair, wiped his fingers on his shirt, arranged his beard, and started in.

"I haven't seen you lately, son. Tell me what you have been doing with yourself." Before Hugh could reply he went on: "No, don't tell me—I will tell you. For one thing you have been exploring, climbing, without too much respect for the forbidden areas. Is it not so?" He held the young man's eye. Hugh fumbled for a reply.

But he was let off again. "Never mind. I know, and you know that I know. I am not too displeased. But it has brought it forcibly to my attention that it is time that you decided what you are to do with your life. Have you any plans?"

"Well—no definite ones, sir."

"How about that girl, Edris Baxter? D'you intend to marry her?"

"Why—uh—I don't know, sir. I guess I want to, and her father is willing, I think. Only—"

"Only what?"

"Well—he wants me to apprentice to his farm. I suppose it's a good idea. His farm together with my uncle's business would make a good property."

"But you're not sure?"

"Well—I don't know."

"Correct. You're not for that. I have other plans. Tell me, have you ever wondered why I taught you to read and write? Of course, you have. But you've kept your own counsel. That is good.

"Now attend me. I've watched you since you were a small child. You have more imagination than the common run, more curiosity, more go. And you are a born leader. You were different even as a baby. Your head was too large, for one thing, and there were some who voted at your birth inspection to put you at once into the Converter. But I held them off. I wanted to see how you would turn out.

"A peasant life is not for the likes of you. You are to be a scientist."

The old man paused and studied his face. Hugh was confused, speechless. Nelson went on: "Oh, yes. Yes, indeed. For a man of your temperament, there are only two things to do with him: Make him one of the custodians, or send him to the Converter."

"Do you mean, sir, that I have nothing to say about it?"

"If you want to put it that bluntly—yes. To leave the bright ones among the ranks of the Crew is to breed heresy. We can't have that. We had it once and it almost destroyed the human race. You have marked yourself out by your exceptional ability; you must now be instructed in right thinking, be initiated into the mysteries, in order that you may be a conserving force rather than a focus of infection and a source of trouble."

The orderly reappeared loaded down with bundles which he dumped on the deck. Hugh glanced at them, then burst out, "Why, those are my things!"

"Certainly," acknowledged Nelson. "I sent for them. You're to sleep here henceforth. I'll see you later and start you on your studies—unless you have something more on your mind?"

"Why, no, sir. I guess not. I must admit I am a little confused. I suppose—I suppose this means you don't want me to marry?"

"Oh, *that*," Nelson answered indifferently. "Take her if you like—her father can't protest now. But let me warn you you'll grow tired of her."

Hugh Hoyland devoured the ancient books that his mentor permitted him to read, and felt no desire for many, many sleeps to go climbing, or even to stir out of Nelson's cabin. More than once he felt that he was on the track of the secret—a secret as yet undefined, even as a question— but again he would find himself more confused than ever. It was evidently harder to reach the wisdom of scientisthood than he had thought.

Once, while he was worrying away at the curious twisted characters of the ancients and trying to puzzle out their odd rhetoric and unfamiliar terms, Nelson came into the little compartment that had been set aside for him, and, laying a fatherly hand on his shoulder, asked, "How goes it, boy?"

"Why, well enough, sir, I suppose," he answered, laying

the book aside. "Some of it is not quite clear to me—not clear at all, to tell the truth."

"That is to be expected," the old man said equably. "I've let you struggle along by yourself at first in order that you may see the traps that native wit alone will fall into. Many of these things are not to be understood without instruction. What have you there?" He picked up the book and glanced at it. It was inscribed *Basic Modern Physics*. "So? This is one of the most valuable of the sacred writings, yet the uninitiate could not possibly make good use of it without help. The first thing that you must understand, my boy, is that our forefathers, for all their spiritual perfection, did not look at things in the fashion in which we do.

"They were incurable romantics, rather than rationalists, as we are, and the truths which they handed down to us, though strictly true, were frequently clothed in allegorical language. For example, have you come to the Law of Gravitation?"

"I read about it."

"Did you understand it? No, I can see that you didn't."

"Well," said Hugh defensively, "it didn't seem to *mean* anything. It just sounded silly, if you will pardon me, sir."

"That illustrates my point. You were thinking of it in literal terms, like the laws governing electrical devices found elsewhere in this same book. 'Two bodies attract each other directly as the product of their masses and inversely as the square of their distance.' It sounds like a rule for simple physical facts, does it not? Yet it is nothing of the sort; it was the poetical way the old ones had of expressing the rule of propinquity which governs the emotion of love. The bodies referred to are human bodies, mass is their capacity for love. Young people have a greater capacity for love than the elderly; when they are thrown together, they fall in love, yet when they are separated they soon get over it. 'Out of sight, out of mind.' It's as simple as that. But you were seeking some deep meaning for it."

Hugh grinned. "I never thought of looking at it that way. I can see that I am going to need a lot of help."

"Is there anything else bothering you just now?"

"Well, yes, lots of things, though I probably can't

remember them offhand. I mind one thing: Tell me, Father, can muties be considered as being people?"

"I can see you have been listening to idle talk. The answer to that is both yes and no. It is true that the muties originally descended from people but they are no longer part of the Crew—they cannot now be considered as members of the human race, for they have flouted Jordan's Law.

"This is a broad subject," he went on, settling down to it. "There is even some question as to the original meaning of the word 'mutie.' Certainly they number among their ancestors the mutineers who escaped death at the time of the rebellion. But they also have in their blood the blood of many of the mutants who were born during the dark age. You understand, of course, that during that period our present wise rule of inspecting each infant for the mark of sin and returning to the Converter any who are found to be mutations was not in force. There are strange and horrible things crawling through the dark passageways and lurking in the deserted levels."

Hugh thought about it for a while, then asked, "Why is it that mutations still show up among us, the people?"

"That is simple. The seed of sin is still in us. From time to time it still shows up, incarnate. In destroying those monsters we help to cleanse the stock and thereby bring closer the culmination of Jordan's Plan, the end of the Trip at our heavenly home, Far Centaurus."

Hoyland's brow wrinkled again. "That is another thing that I don't understand. Many of these ancient writings speak of the Trip as if it were an actual *moving,* a going-somewhere—as if the Ship itself were no more than a pushcart. How can that be?"

Nelson chuckled. "How can it, indeed? How can that move which is the background against which all else moves? The answer, of course, is plain. You have again mistaken allegorical language for the ordinary usage of everyday speech. Of course, the Ship is solid, immovable, in a physical sense. How can the whole universe move? Yet, it *does* move, in a spiritual sense. With every righteous act we move closer to the sublime destination of Jordan's Plan."

Hugh nodded. "I think I see."

"Of course, it is conceivable that Jordan could have fashioned the world in some other shape than the Ship, had it suited His purpose. When man was younger and more poetical, holy men vied with one another in inventing fanciful worlds which Jordan might have created. One school invented an entire mythology of a topsy-turvy world of endless reaches of space, empty save for pinpoints of light and bodiless mythological monsters. They called it the heavenly world, or heaven, as if to contrast it with the solid reality of the Ship. They seemed never to tire of speculating about it, inventing details for it, and of making pictures of what they conceived it to be like. I suppose they did it to the greater glory of Jordan, and who is to say that He found their dreams unacceptable? But in this modern age we have more serious work to do."

Hugh was not interested in astronomy. Even his untutored mind had been able to see in its wild extravagance an intention not literal. He turned to problems nearer at hand.

"Since the muties are the seed of sin, why do we make no effort to wipe them out? Would not that be an act that would speed the Plan?"

The old man considered a while before replying. "That is a fair question and deserves a straight answer. Since you are to be a scientist you will need to know the answer. Look at it this way: There is a definite limit to the number of Crew the Ship can support. If our numbers increase without limit, there comes a time when there will not be good eating for all of us. Is it not better that some should die in brushes with the muties than that we should grow in numbers until we killed each other for food?

"The ways of Jordan are inscrutable. Even the muties have a part in His Plan."

It seemed reasonable, but Hugh was not sure.

But when Hugh was transferred to active work as a junior scientist in the operation of the Ship's functions, he found there were other opinions. As was customary, he put in a period serving the Converter. The work was not onerous; he had principally to check in the waste materials brought in by porters from each of the villages, keep books of their contributions, and make sure that no reclaimable metal was introduced into the first-stage hopper. But it brought him into contact with Bill Ertz, the Assistant Chief Engineer, a man not much older than himself.

He discussed with him the things he had learned from Nelson, and was shocked at Ertz's attitude.

"Get this through your head, kid," Ertz told him. "This is a practical job for practical men. Forget all that romantic nonsense. Jordan's Plan! That stuff is all right to keep the peasants quiet and in their place, but don't fall for it yourself. There is no Plan—other than our own plans for looking out for ourselves. The Ship has to have light and heat and power for cooking and irrigation. The Crew can't get along without those things and that makes us boss of the Crew.

"As for this softheaded tolerance toward the muties, you're going to see some changes made! Keep your mouth shut and string along with us."

It impressed on him that he was expected to maintain a primary loyalty to the bloc of younger men among the scientists. They were a well-knit organization within an organization and were made up of practical, hardheaded men who were working toward improvement of conditions throughout the Ship, as they saw them. They were well-knit because an apprentice who failed to see things their way did not last long. Either he failed to measure up and soon found himself back in the ranks of the peasants, or, as was more likely, suffered some mishap and wound up in the Converter.

And Hoyland began to see that they were right.

They were realists. The Ship was the Ship. It was a fact, requiring no explanation. As for Jordan—who had ever seen Him, spoken to Him? What was this nebulous Plan of His? The object of life was living. A man was born, lived his life, and then went to the Converter. It was as simple as that, no mystery to it, no sublime Trip and no Centaurus. These romantic stories were simply hangovers from the childhood of the race before men gained the understanding and the courage to look facts in the face.

He ceased bothering his head about astronomy and mystical physics and all the other mass of mythology he had been taught to revere. He was still amused, more or less, by the Lines from the Beginning and by all the old

stories about Earth—what the Huff was "Earth," anyhow?
—but now realized that such things could be taken seriously only by children and dullards.

Besides, there was work to do. The younger men, while
still maintaining the nominal authority of their elders, had
plans of their own, the first of which was a systematic
extermination of the muties. Beyond that, their intentions
were still fluid, but they contemplated making full use of
the resources of the Ship, including the upper levels. The
young men were able to move ahead with their plans without an open breach with their elders because the older
scientists simply did not bother to any great extent with
the routine of the Ship. The present Captain had grown so
fat that he rarely stirred from his cabin; his aide, one of
the young men's bloc, attended to affairs for him.

Hoyland never laid eyes on the Chief Engineer save
once, when he showed up for the purely religious ceremony
of manning landing stations.

The project of cleaning out the muties required reconnaissance of the upper levels to be done systematically.
It was in carrying out such scouting that Hugh Hoyland was
again ambushed by a mutie.

This mutie was more accurate with his slingshot.
Hoyland's companions, forced to retreat by superior
numbers, left him for dead.

Joe-Jim Gregory was playing himself a game of checkers.
Time was when they had played cards together, but Joe,
the head on the right, had suspected Jim, the left-hand
member of the team, of cheating. They had quarreled about
it, then given it up, for they both learned early in their joint
career that two heads on one pair of shoulders must
necessarily find ways of getting along together.

Checkers was better. They could both see the board,
and disagreement was impossible.

A loud metallic knocking at the door of the compartment
interrupted the game. Joe-Jim unsheathed his throwing
knife and cradled it, ready for quick use. "Come in!"
roared Jim.

The door opened, the one who had knocked backed into
the room—the only safe way, as everyone knew, to enter
Joe-Jim's presence. The newcomer was squat and ruggedly

powerful, not over four feet in height. The relaxed body of a man hung across one shoulder and was steadied by a hand.

Joe-Jim returned the knife to its sheath. "Put it down, Bobo," Jim ordered.

"And close the door," added Joe. "Now what have we got here?"

It was a young man, apparently dead, though no wound appeared on him. Bobo patted a thigh. "Eat 'im?" he said hopefully. Saliva spilled out of his still-opened lips.

"Maybe," temporized Jim. "Did you kill him?"

Bobo shook his undersized head.

"Good Bobo," Joe approved. "Where did you hit him?"

"Bobo hit him *there*." The microcephalic shoved a broad thumb against the supine figure in the area between the umbilicus and the breastbone.

"Good shot," Joe approved. "We couldn't have done better with a knife."

"Bobo *good* shot," the dwarf agreed blandly. "Want see?" He twitched his slingshot invitingly.

"Shut up," answered Joe, not unkindly. "No, we don't want to see; we want to make him talk."

"Bobo fix," the short one agreed, and started with simple brutality to carry out his purpose.

Joe-Jim slapped him away, and applied other methods, painful but considerably less drastic than those of the dwarf. The younger man jerked and opened his eyes.

"Eat 'im?" repeated Bobo.

"No," said Joe. "When did you eat last?" inquired Jim.

Bobo shook his head and rubbed his stomach, indicating with graphic pantomime that it had been a long time—too long. Joe-Jim went over to a locker, opened it, and withdrew a haunch of meat. He held it up. Jim smelled it and Joe drew his head away in nose-wrinkling disgust. Joe-Jim threw it to Bobo, who snatched it happily out of the air. "Now, get out," ordered Jim.

Bobo trotted away, closing the door behind him. Joe-Jim turned to the captive and prodded him with his foot. "Speak up," said Jim. "Who the Huff are you?"

The young man shivered, put a hand to his head, then seemed suddenly to bring his surroundings into focus, for he scrambled to his feet, moving awkwardly against the low weight conditions of this level, and reached for his knife.

It was not at his belt.

Joe-Jim had his own out and brandished it. "Be good and you won't get hurt. What do they call you?"

The young man wet his lips, and his eyes hurried about the room. "Speak up," said Joe.

"Why bother with him?" inquired Jim. "I'd say he was only good for meat. Better call Bobo back."

"No hurry about that," Joe answered. "I want to talk to him. What's your name?"

The prisoner looked again at the knife and muttered, "Hugh Hoyland."

"That doesn't tell us much," Jim commented. "What d'you do? What village do you come from? And what were you doing in mutie country?"

But this time Hoyland was sullen. Even the prick of the knife against his ribs caused him only to bite his lips. "Shucks," said Joe, "he's only a stupid peasant. Let's drop it."

"Shall we finish him off?"

"No. Not now. Shut him up."

Joe-Jim opened the door of a small side compartment, and urged Hugh in with the knife. He then closed and fastened the door and went back to his game. "Your move, Jim."

The compartment in which Hugh was locked was dark. He soon satisfied himself by touch that the smooth steel walls were entirely featureless save for the solid, securely fastened door. Presently he lay down on the deck and gave himself up to fruitless thinking.

He had plenty of time to think, time to fall asleep and awaken more than once. And time to grow very hungry and very, very thirsty.

When Joe-Jim next took sufficient interest in his prisoner to open the door of the cell, Hoyland was not immediately in evidence. He had planned many times what he would do when the door opened and his chance came, but when the event arrived, he was too weak, semi-comatose. Joe-Jim dragged him out.

The disturbance roused him to partial comprehension. He sat up and stared around him.

"Ready to talk?" asked Jim.

Hoyland opened his mouth but no words came out.

"Can't you see he's too dry to talk?" Joe told his twin. Then to Hugh: "Will you talk if we give you some water?"

Hoyland looked puzzled, then nodded vigorously.

Joe-Jim returned in a moment with a mug of water. Hugh drank greedily, paused, and seemed about to faint.

Joe-Jim took the mug from him. "That's enough for now," said Joe. "Tell us about yourself."

Hugh did so. In detail, being prompted from time to time.

Hugh accepted a *de facto* condition of slavery with no particular resistance and no great disturbance of soul. The word "slave" was not in his vocabulary, but the condition was a commonplace in everything he had ever known. There had always been those who gave orders and those who carried them out—he could imagine no other condition, no other type of social organization. It was a fact of nature.

Though naturally he thought of escape.

Thinking about it was as far as he got. Joe-Jim guessed his thoughts and brought the matter out into the open. Joe told him, "Don't go getting ideas, youngster. Without a knife you wouldn't get three levels away in this part of the Ship. If you managed to steal a knife from me, you still wouldn't make it down to high-weight. Besides, there's Bobo."

Hugh waited a moment, as was fitting, then said, "Bobo?"

Jim grinned and replied, "We told Bobo that you were his to butcher, if he liked, if you ever stuck your head out of our compartments without us. Now he sleeps outside the door and spends a lot of his time there."

"It was only fair," put in Joe. "He was disappointed when we decided to keep you."

"Say," suggested Jim, turning his head toward his brother's, "how about some fun?" He turned back to Hugh. "Can you throw a knife?"

"Of course," Hugh answered.

"Let's see you. Here." Joe-Jim handed him their own knife. Hugh accepted it, jiggling it in his hand to try its balance. "Try my mark."

Joe-Jim had a plastic target set up at the far end of the room from his favorite chair, on which he was wont to practice his own skill. Hugh eyed it, and, with an arm motion too fast to follow, let fly. He used the economical underhand stroke, thumb on the blade, fingers together.

The blade shivered in the target, well centered in the chewed-up area which marked Joe-Jim's best efforts.

"Good boy!" Joe approved. "What do you have in mind, Jim?"

"Let's give him the knife and see how far he gets."

"No," said Joe, "I don't agree."

"Why not?"

"If Bobo wins, we're out one servant. If Hugh wins, we lose both Bobo and him. It's wasteful."

"Oh, well—if you insist."

"I do. Hugh, fetch the knife."

Hugh did so. It had not occurred to him to turn the knife against Joe-Jim. The master was the master. For servant to attack master was not simply repugnant to good morals, it was an idea so wild that it did not occur to him at all.

Hugh had expected that Joe-Jim would be impressed by his learning as a scientist. It did not work out that way. Joe-Jim, especially Jim, loved to argue. They sucked Hugh dry in short order and figuratively cast him aside. Hoyland felt humiliated. After all, was he not a scientist? Could he not read and write?

"Shut up," Jim told him. "Reading is simple. I could do it before your father was born. D'you think you're the first scientist that has served me? Scientists—bah! A pack of ignoramuses!"

In an attempt to re-establish his own intellectual conceit, Hugh expounded the theories of the younger scientists, the strictly matter-of-fact, hard-boiled realism which rejected all religious interpretation and took the Ship as it was. He confidently expected Joe-Jim to approve such a point of view; it seemed to fit their temperaments.

They laughed in his face.

"Honest," Jim insisted, when he had ceased snorting, "are you young punks so stupid as all that? Why, you're worse than your elders."

"But you just got through saying," Hugh protested in hurt tones, "that all our accepted religious notions are so much bunk. That is just what my friends think. They want to junk all that old nonsense."

Joe started to speak; Jim cut in ahead of him. "Why bother with him, Joe? He's hopeless."

"No, he's not. I'm enjoying this. He's the first one I've talked with in I don't know how long who stood any chance at all of seeing the truth. Let us be—I want to see whether that's a head he has on his shoulders, or just a place to hang his ears."

"O.K.," Jim agreed, "but keep it quiet. I'm going to take a nap." The left-hand head closed its eyes, soon it was snoring. Joe and Hugh continued their discussion in whispers.

"The trouble with you youngsters," Joe said, "is that if you can't understand a thing right off, you think it can't be true. The trouble with your elders is, anything they didn't understand they reinterpreted to mean something else and then thought they understood it. None of you has tried believing clear words the way they were written and then tried to understand them on that basis. Oh, no, you're all too bloody smart for that—if you can't see it right off, it ain't so—it must mean something different."

"What do you mean?" Hugh asked suspiciously.

"Well, take the Trip, for instance. What does it mean to you?"

"Well—to my mind, it doesn't mean anything. It's just a piece of nonsense to impress the peasants."

"And what is the accepted meaning?"

"Well—it's where you go when you die—or rather what you do. You make the Trip to Centaurus."

"And what is Centaurus?"

"It's—mind you, I'm just telling you the orthodox answers; I don't really believe this stuff—it's where you arrive when you've made the Trip, a place where everybody's happy and there's always good eating."

Joe snorted. Jim broke the rhythm of his snoring, opened one eye, and settled back again with a grunt.

"That's just what I mean," Joe went on in a lower whisper. "You don't use your head. Did it ever occur to you that the Trip was just what the old books said it was—the Ship and all the Crew actually going somewhere, moving?"

Hoyland thought about it. "You don't mean for me to take you seriously. Physically, it's an impossibility. The Ship can't *go* anywhere. It already *is* everywhere. We can make a trip through it, but *the* Trip—that has to have a spiritual meaning, if it has any."

Joe called on Jordan to support him. "Now, listen," he said, "get this through that thick head of yours. Imagine a place a lot bigger than the Ship, a lot bigger, with the Ship inside it—*moving*. D'you get it?"

Hugh tried. He tried very hard. He shook his head. "It doesn't make sense," he said. "There can't be anything bigger than the Ship. There wouldn't be any place for it to *be*."

"Oh, for Huff's sake! Listen—*outside* the Ship, get that? Straight down beyond the level in every direction. Emptiness out there. Understand me?"

"But there isn't anything below the lowest level. That's why it's the lowest level."

"Look. If you took a knife and started digging a hole in the floor of the lowest level, where would it get you?"

"But you *can't*. It's too hard."

"But suppose you did and it made a hole. Where would that hole go? Imagine it."

Hugh shut his eyes and tried to imagine digging a hole in the lowest level. Digging—as if it were soft—soft as cheese.

He began to get some glimmering of a possibility, a possibility that was unsettling, soul-shaking. He was falling, falling into a hole that he had dug which had no levels under it. He opened his eyes very quickly. "That's awful!" he ejaculated. "I won't believe it."

Joe-Jim got up. "I'll *make* you believe it," he said grimly, "if I have to break your neck to do it." He strode over to the outer door and opened it. "Bobo!" he shouted. "Bobo!"

Jim's head snapped erect. "Wassa matter? Wha's going on?"

"We're going to take Hugh to no-weight."

"What for?"

"To pound some sense into his silly head."

"Some other time."

"No, I want to do it now."

"All right, all right. No need to shake. I'm awake now, anyhow."

Joe-Jim Gregory was almost as nearly unique in his, or their, mental ability as he was in his bodily construction. Under any circumstances he would have been a dominant personality; among the muties it was inevitable that he should bully them, order them about, and live on their services. Had he had the will-to-power, it is conceivable that he could have organized the muties to fight and overcome the Crew proper.

But he lacked that drive. He was by native temperament an intellectual, a bystander, an observer. He was interested in the "how" and the "why," but his will to action was satisfied with comfort and convenience alone.

Had he been born two normal twins and among the Crew, it is likely that he would have drifted into sci-entisthood as the easiest and most satisfactory answer to the problem of living and as such would have entertained himself mildly with conversation and administration. As it was, he lacked mental companionship and had whiled away three generations reading and rereading books stolen for him by his stooges.

The two halves of his dual person had argued and discussed what they had read, and had almost inevitably arrived at a reasonably coherent theory of history and the physical world—except in one respect, the concept of fiction was entirely foreign to them; they treated the novels that had been provided for the Jordan expedition in exactly the same fashion that they did text and reference books.

This led to their one major difference of opinion. Jim regarded Allan Quartermain as the greatest man who had ever lived; Joe held out for John Henry.

They were both inordinately fond of poetry; they could recite page after page of Kipling, and were nearly as fond of Rhysling, "the blind singer of the spaceways."

Bobo backed in. Joe-Jim hooked a thumb toward Hugh. "Look," said Joe, "he's going out."

"Now?" said Bobo happily, and grinned, slavering.

"You and your stomach!" Joe answered, rapping Bobo's pate with his knuckles. "No, you don't eat him. You and him—blood brothers. Get it?"

"Not eat 'im?"

"No. Fight for him. He fights for you."

"O.K." The pinhead shrugged his shoulders at the inevitable. "Blood brothers. Bobo know."

"All right. Now we go up to the place-where-everybody-flies. You go ahead and make lookout."

They climbed in single file, the dwarf running ahead to spot the lie of the land, Hoyland behind him, Joe-Jim bringing up the rear, Joe with eyes to the front, Jim watching their rear, head turned over his shoulder.

Higher and higher they went, weight slipping imperceptibly from them with each successive deck. They emerged finally into a level beyond which there was no further progress, no opening above them. The deck curved gently, suggesting that the true shape of the space was a giant cylinder, but overhead a metallic expanse which exhibited a similar curvature obstructed the view and prevented one from seeing whether or not the deck in truth curved back on itself.

There were no proper bulkheads; great stanchions, so huge and squat as to give an impression of excessive, unnecessary strength, grew thickly about them, spacing deck and overhead evenly apart.

Weight was imperceptible. If one remained quietly in one place, the undetectable residuum of weight would bring the body in a gentle drift down to the "floor," but "up" and "down" were terms largely lacking in meaning. Hugh did not like it; it made him gulp, but Bobo seemed delighted by it and not unused to it. He moved through the air like an uncouth fish, banking off stanchion, floor plate, and overhead as suited his convenience.

Joe-Jim set a course parallel to the common axis of the inner and outer cylinders, following a passageway formed by the orderly spacing of the stanchions. There were handrails set along the passage, one of which he followed like a spider on its thread. He made remarkable speed, which Hugh floundered to maintain. In time, he caught the trick of the easy, effortless, overhand pull, the long coast against nothing but air resistance, and the occasional flick of the toes or the hand against the floor. But he was much too busy to tell how far they went before they stopped. Miles, he guessed it to be, but he did not know.

When they did stop, it was because the passage had terminated. A solid bulkhead, stretching away to right and left, barred their way. Joe-Jim moved along it to the right, searching.

He found what he sought, a man-sized door, closed, its presence distinguishable only by a faint crack which marked its outline and a cursive geometrical design on its surface. Joe-Jim studied this and scratched his right-hand head. The two heads whispered to each other. Joe-Jim raised his hand in an awkward gesture.

"No, no!" said Jim. Joe-Jim checked himself. "How's that?" Joe answered. They whispered together again, Joe nodded, and Joe-Jim again raised his hand.

He traced the design on the door without touching it, moving his forefinger through the air perhaps four inches from the surface of the door. The order of succession in which his finger moved over the lines of the design appeared simple but certainly not obvious.

Finished, he shoved a palm against the adjacent bulkhead, drifted back from the door, and waited.

A moment later there was a soft, almost inaudible insufflation; the door stirred and moved outward perhaps six inches, then stopped. Joe-Jim appeared puzzled. He ran his hands cautiously into the open crack and pulled. Nothing happened. He called to Bobo, "Open it."

Bobo looked the situation over, with a scowl on his forehead which wrinkled almost to his crown. He then placed his feet against the bulkhead, steadying himself by grasping the door with one hand. He took hold of the edge of the door with both hands, settled his feet firmly, bowed his body, and strained.

He held his breath, chest rigid, back bent, sweat breaking out from the effort. The great cords in his neck stood out, making of his head a misshapen pyramid. Hugh could hear the dwarf's joints crack. It was easy to believe that he would kill himself with the attempt, too stupid to give up.

But the door gave suddenly, with a plaint of binding metal. As the door, in swinging out, slipped from Bobo's fingers, the unexpectedly released tension in his legs shoved him heavily away from the bulkhead; he plunged down the passageway, floundering for a handhold. But he was back in a moment, drifting awkwardly through the air as he massaged a cramped calf.

Joe-Jim led the way inside, Hugh close behind him. "What is this place?" demanded Hugh, his curiosity overcoming his servant manners.

"The Main Control Room," said Joe.

Main Control Room! The most sacred and taboo place in the Ship, its very location a forgotten mystery. In the credo of the young men it was nonexistent. The older scientists varied in their attitude between fundamentalist acceptance and mystical belief. As enlightened as Hugh believed himself to be, the very words frightened him. The Control Room! Why, the very spirit of Jordan was said to reside there.

He stopped.

Joe-Jim stopped and Joe looked around. "Come on," he said. "What's the matter?"

"Why—uh—uh—"

"Speak up."

"But—but this place is haunted—this is Jordan's—"

"Oh, for Jordan's sake!" protested Joe, with slow exasperation. "I thought you told me you young punks didn't take any stock in Jordan."

"Yes, but—but this is—"

"Stow it. Come along, or I'll have Bobo drag you." He turned away. Hugh followed, reluctantly, as a man climbs a scaffold.

They threaded through a passageway just wide enough for two to use the handrails abreast. The passage curved in a wide sweeping arc of full ninety degrees, then opened into the control room proper. Hugh peered past Joe-Jim's broad shoulders, fearful but curious.

He stared into a well-lighted room, huge, quite two hundred feet across. It was spherical, the interior of a great globe. The surface of the globe was featureless, frosted silver. In the geometrical center of the sphere Hugh saw a group of apparatus about fifteen feet across. To his inexperienced eye, it was completely unintelligible; he could not have described it, but he saw that it floated steadily, with no apparent support.

Running from the end of the passage to the mass at the center of the globe was a tube of metal latticework, wide as the passage itself. It offered the only exit from the passage. Joe-Jim turned to Bobo, and ordered him to remain in the passageway, then entered the tube.

He pulled himself along it, hand over hand, the bars of the latticework making a ladder. Hugh followed him; they emerged into the mass of apparatus occupying the center of the sphere. Seen close up, the gear of the control station resolved itself into its individual details, but it still made no sense to him. He glanced away from it to the inner surface of the globe which surrounded them.

That was a mistake. The surface of the globe, being featureless silvery white, had nothing to lend it perspective. It might have been a hundred feet away, or a thousand, or many miles. He had never experienced an unbroken height greater than that between two decks, nor an open space larger than the village common. He was panic-stricken, scared out of his wits, the more so in that he did not know what it was he feared. But the ghost of long-forgotten jungle ancestors possessed him and chilled his stomach with the basic primitive fear of falling.

He clutched at the control gear, clutched at Joe-Jim.

Joe-Jim let him have one, hard across the mouth with the flat of his hand. "What's the matter with you?" growled Jim.

"I don't know," Hugh presently managed to get out. "I don't know, but I don't *like* this place. Let's get out of here!"

Jim lifted his eyebrows to Joe, looked disgusted, and said, "We might as well. That weak-bellied baby will never understand anything you tell him."

"Oh, he'll be all right," Joe replied, dismissing the matter. "Hugh, climb into one of the chairs—there, that one."

In the meantime, Hugh's eyes had fallen on the tube whereby they had reached the control center and had followed it back by eye to the passage door. The sphere suddenly shrank to its proper focus and the worst of his panic was over. He complied with the order, still trembling, but able to obey.

The control center consisted of a rigid framework, made up of chairs, or frames, to receive the bodies of the operators, and consolidated instrument and report panels, mounted in such a fashion as to be almost in the laps of the operators, where they were readily visible but did not obstruct the view. The chairs had high supporting sides, or arms, and mounted in these arms were the controls appropriate to each officer on watch—but Hugh was not yet aware of that.

He slid under the instrument panel into his seat and settled back, glad of its enfolding stability. It fitted him in a semi-reclining position, footrest to head support.

But something was happening on the panel in front of Joe-Jim; he caught it out of the corner of his eye and turned to look. Bright red letters glowed near the top of the board: 2ND ASTROGATOR POSTED. What was a second astrogator? He didn't know—then he noticed that the extreme top of his own board was labeled 2ND ASTROGATOR and concluded it must be himself, or rather, the man who should be sitting there. He felt momentarily uncomfortable that the proper second astrogator might come in and find him usurping his post, but he put it out of his mind—it seemed unlikely.

But what was a second astrogator, anyhow?

The letters faded from Joe-Jim's board, a red dot appeared on the left-hand edge and remained. Joe-Jim did something with his right hand; his board reported: ACCELERATION—ZERO, then MAIN DRIVE. The last two words blinked several times, then were replaced with NO REPORT. These words faded out, and a bright green dot appeared near the right-hand edge.

"Get ready," said Joe, looking toward Hugh; "the light is going out."

"You're not going to turn out the light?" protested Hugh.

"No—you are. Take a look by your left hand. See those little white lights?"

Hugh did so, and found, shining up through the surface

of the chair arm, eight bright little beads of light arranged
in two squares, one above the other.

"Each one controls the light of one quadrant," explained
Joe. "Cover them with your hand to turn out the light.
Go ahead—do it."

Reluctantly, but fascinated, Hugh did as he was directed. He placed a palm over the tiny lights, and waited.
The silvery sphere turned to dull lead, faded still more,
leaving them in darkness complete save for the silent glow
from the instrument panels. Hugh felt nervous but ex-
hilarated. He withdrew his palm; the sphere remained dark,
the eight little lights had turned blue.

"Now," said Joe, "I'm going to show you the stars!"

In the darkness, Joe-Jim's right hand slid over another
pattern of eight lights.

Creation.

Faithfully reproduced, shining as steady and serene
from the walls of the stellarium as did their originals from
the black deeps of space, the mirrored stars looked down
on him. Light after jeweled light, scattered in careless
bountiful splendor across the simulacrum sky, the countless suns lay before him—before him, over him, under him,
behind him, in every direction from him. He hung alone
in the center of the stellar universe.

"Oooooh!" It was an involuntary sound, caused by his
indrawn breath. He clutched the chair arms hard enough
to break fingernails, but he was not aware of it. Nor was
he afraid at the moment; there was room in his being for
but one emotion. Life within the Ship, alternately harsh
and workaday, had placed no strain on his innate capacity
to experience beauty; for the first time in his life he knew
the intolerable ecstasy of beauty unalloyed. It shook him
and hurt him, like the first trembling intensity of sex.

It was some time before Hugh sufficiently recovered from
the shock and the ensuing intense preoccupation to be
able to notice Jim's sardonic laugh, Joe's dry chuckle.
"Had enough?" inquired Joe. Without waiting for a reply,
Joe-Jim turned the lights back on, using the duplicate
controls mounted in the left arm of his chair.

Hugh sighed. His chest ached and his heart pounded.
He realized suddenly that he had been holding his breath

he entire time that the lights had been turned out. "Well, smart boy," asked Jim, "are you convinced?"

Hugh sighed again, not knowing why. With the lights back on, he felt safe and snug again, but was possessed of a deep sense of personal loss. He knew, subconsciously, that, having seen the stars, he would never be happy again. The dull ache in his breast, the vague inchoate yearning for his lost heritage of open sky and stars, was never to be silenced, even though he was yet too ignorant to be aware of it at the top of his mind. "What was it?" he asked in a hushed voice.

"That's *it*," answered Joe. "That's the world. That's the universe. That's what I've been trying to tell you about."

Hugh tried furiously to force his inexperienced mind to comprehend. "That's what you mean by Outside?" he asked. "All those beautiful little lights?"

"Sure," said Joe, "only they aren't little. They're a long way off, you see—maybe thousands of miles."

"What?"

"Sure, sure," Joe persisted. "There's lots of room out here. Space. It's big. Why, some of those stars may be as big as the Ship—maybe bigger."

Hugh's face was a pitiful study in overstrained imagination. "Bigger than the Ship?" he repeated. "But —but—"

Jim tossed his head impatiently and said to Joe, "Wha'd' I tell you? You're wasting our time on this lunk. He hasn't got the capacity—"

"Easy, Jim," Joe answered mildly; "don't expect him to run before he can crawl. It took us a long time. I seem to remember that you were a little slow to believe your own eyes."

"That's a lie," said Jim nastily. "*You* were the one that had to be convinced."

"O.K., O.K.," Joe conceded; "let it ride. But it was a long time before we both had it all straight."

Hoyland paid little attention to the exchange between the two brothers. It was a usual thing; his attention was centered on matters decidedly not usual. "Joe," he asked, "what became of the Ship while we were looking at the stars? Did we stare right through it?"

"Not exactly," Joe told him. "You weren't looking directly at the stars at all, but at a kind of picture of them. It's like— Well, they do it with mirrors, sort of. I've got a book that tells about it."

"But you *can* see 'em directly," volunteered Jim, his momentary pique forgotten. "There's a compartment forward of here—"

"Oh, yes," put in Joe, "it slipped my mind. The Captain's veranda. 'S got one all of glass; you can look right out."

"The Captain's veranda? But—"

"Not *this* Captain. He's never been near the place. That's the name over the door of the compartment."

"What's a 'veranda'?"

"Blessed if I know. It's just the name of the place."

"Will you take me up there?"

Joe appeared to be about to agree, but Jim cut in. "Some other time. I want to get back—I'm hungry."

They passed back through the tube, woke up Bobo, and made the long trip back down.

It was long before Hugh could persuade Joe-Jim to take him exploring again, but the time intervening was well spent. Joe-Jim turned him loose on the largest collection of books that Hugh had ever seen. Some of them were copies of books Hugh had seen before, but even these he read with new meanings. He read incessantly, his mind soaking up new ideas, stumbling over them, struggling, striving to grasp them. He begrudged sleep, he forgot to eat until his breath grew sour and compelling pain in his midriff forced him to pay attention to his body. Hunger satisfied, he would be back at it until his head ached and his eyes refused to focus.

Joe-Jim's demands for service were few. Although Hugh was never off duty, Joe-Jim did not mind his reading as long as he was within earshot and ready to jump when called. Playing checkers with one of the pair when the other did not care to play was the service which used up the most time, and even this was not a total loss, for, if the player were Joe, he could almost always be diverted into a discussion of the Ship, its history, its machinery and equipment, the sort of people who had built it and first

manned it— and *their* history, back on Earth, Earth the
incredible, that strange place where people had lived on
the *outside* instead of the *inside*.

Hugh wondered why they did not fall off.

He took the matter up with Joe and at last gained some
notion of gravitation. He never really understood it
emotionally—it was too wildly improbable—but as an
intellectual concept he was able to accept it and use it, much
later, in his first vague glimmerings of the science of
ballistics and the art of astrogation and ship maneuvering.
And it led in time to his wondering about weight in the
Ship, a matter that had never bothered him before. The
lower the level the greater the weight had been to his mind
imply the order of nature, and nothing to wonder at. He
was familiar with centrifugal force as it applied to
slingshots. To apply it also to the whole Ship, to think of
the Ship as spinning like a slingshot and thereby causing
weight, was too much of a hurdle—he never really believed
it.

Joe-Jim took him back once more to the Control Room
and showed him what little Joe-Jim knew about the
manipulation of the controls and the reading of the astrogation instruments.

The long-forgotten engineer-designers employed by the
Jordan Foundation had been instructed to design a ship
that would not—*could* not—wear out, even though the
trip were protracted beyond the expected sixty years. They
builded better than they knew. In planning the main drive
engines and the auxiliary machinery, largely automatic,
which would make the Ship habitable, and in designing
the controls necessary to handle all machinery not entirely
automatic, the very idea of moving parts had been rejected.
The engines and auxiliary equipment worked on a level
below mechanical motion, on a level of pure force, as
electrical transformers do. Instead of push buttons, levers,
cams, and shafts, the controls and the machinery they
served were planned in terms of balance between static
fields, bias of electronic flow, circuits broken or closed by
a hand placed over a light.

On this level of action, friction lost its meaning, wear
and erosion took no toll. Had all hands been killed in
the mutiny, the Ship would still have plunged on through

space, still lighted, its air still fresh and moist, its engines ready and waiting. As it was, though elevators and conveyor belts fell into disrepair, disuse, and finally into the oblivion of forgotten function, the essential machinery of the Ship continued its automatic service to its ignorant human freight, or waited, quiet and ready, for someone bright enough to puzzle out its key.

Genius had gone into the building of the Ship. Far too huge to be assembled on Earth, it had been put together piece by piece in its own orbit out beyond the Moon. There it had swung for fifteen silent years while the problems presented by the decision to make its machinery fool-proof and enduring had been formulated and solved. A whole new field of submolar action had been conceived in the process, struggled with, and conquered.

So— When Hugh placed an untutored, questing hand over the first of a row of lights marked ACCELERATION, POSITIVE, he got an immediate response, though not in terms of acceleration. A red light at the top of the chief pilot's board blinked rapidly and the annunciator panel glowed with a message: MAIN ENGINES—NOT MANNED.

"What does that mean?" he asked Joe-Jim.

"There's no telling," said Jim. "We've done the same thing in the main engine room," added Joe. "There, when you try it, it says 'Control Room Not Manned.' "

Hugh thought a moment. "What would happen," he persisted, "if all the control stations had somebody at 'em at once, and then I did that?"

"Can't say," said Joe. "Never been able to try it."

Hugh said nothing. A resolve which had been growing, formless, in his mind was now crystallizing into decision. He was busy with it.

He waited until he found Joe-Jim in a mellow mood, both of him, before broaching his idea. They were in the Captain's veranda at the time Hugh decided the moment was ripe. Joe-Jim rested gently in the Captain's easy chair, his belly full of food, and gazed out through the heavy glass of the view port at the serene stars. Hugh floated beside him. The spinning of the Ship caused the stars to appear to move in stately circles.

Presently he said, "Joe-Jim—"

"Eh? What's that, youngster?" It was Joe who had replied.

"It's pretty swell, isn't it?"

"What is?"

"All that. The stars." Hugh indicated the view through the port with a sweep of his arm, then caught at the chair to stop his own backspin.

"Yeah, it sure is. Makes you feel good." Surprisingly, it was Jim who offered this.

Hugh knew the time was right. He waited a moment, then said, "Why don't we finish the job?"

Two heads turned simultaneously, Joe leaning out a little to see past Jim. "What job?"

"The Trip. Why don't we start up the main drive and go on with it? Somewhere out there," he said hurriedly to finish before he was interrupted, "there are planets like Earth—or so the First Crew thought. Let's go find them."

Jim looked at him, then laughed. Joe shook his head.

"Kid," he said, "you don't know what you are talking about. You're as balmy as Bobo. No," he went on, "that's all over and done with. Forget it."

"Why is it over and done with, Joe?"

"Well, because— It's too big a job. It takes a crew that understands what it's all about, trained to operate the Ship."

"Does it take so many? You have shown me only about a dozen places, all told, for men actually to be at the controls. Couldn't a dozen men run the Ship—if they knew what you know," he added slyly.

Jim chuckled. "He's got you, Joe. He's right."

Joe brushed it aside. "You overrate our knowledge. Maybe we *could* operate the Ship, but we wouldn't get anywhere. We don't know where we are. The Ship has been drifting for I don't know how many generations. We don't know where we're headed, or how fast we're going."

"But look," Hugh pleaded, "there are instruments. You showed them to me. Couldn't we learn how to use them? Couldn't *you* figure them out, Joe, if you really wanted to?"

"Oh, I suppose so," Jim agreed.

"Don't boast, Jim," said Joe.

"I'm not boasting," snapped Jim. "If a thing'll work, I can figure it out."

"Humph!" said Joe.

The matter rested in delicate balance. Hugh had got them disagreeing among themselves—which was what he wanted—with the less tractable of the pair on his side. Now, to consolidate his gain—

"I had an idea," he said quickly, "to get you men to work with, Jim, if you were able to train them."

"What's your idea?" demanded Jim suspiciously.

"Well, you remember what I told you about a bunch of the younger scientists—"

"Those fools!"

"Yes, yes, sure—but they don't know what you know. In their way they were trying to be reasonable. Now, if I could go back down and tell them what you've taught me, I could get you enough men to work with."

Joe cut in. "Take a good look at us, Hugh. What do you see?"

"Why—why—I see *you*—Joe-Jim."

"You see a mutie," corrected Joe, his voice edged with sarcasm. "We're a *mutie*. Get that? Your scientists won't work with us."

"No, no," protested Hugh, "that's not true. I'm not talking about peasants. Peasants wouldn't understand, but these are *scientists*, and the smartest of the lot. They'll understand. All you need to do is to arrange safe conduct for them through mutie country. You can do that, can't you?" he added, instinctively shifting the point of the argument to firmer ground.

"Why, sure," said Jim.

"Forget it," said Joe.

"Well, O.K.," Hugh agreed, sensing that Joe really was annoyed at his persistence, "but it would be fun—" He withdrew some distance from the brothers.

He could hear Joe-Jim continuing the discussion with himself in low tones. He pretended to ignore it. Joe-Jim had this essential defect in his joint nature: being a committee, rather than a single individual, he was hardly fitted to be a man of action, since all decisions were necessarily the result of discussion and compromise.

Several moments later Hugh heard Joe's voice raised. "All right, all *right*—have it your own way!" He then called out, "Hugh! Come here!"

Hugh kicked himself away from an adjacent bulkhead and shot over to the immediate vicinity of Joe-Jim, arresting his flight with both hands against the framework of the Captain's chair.

"We've decided," said Joe without preliminaries, "to let you go back down to the high-weight and try to peddle your goods. But you're a fool," he added sourly.

Bobo escorted Hugh down through the dangers of the levels frequented by muties and left him in the uninhabited zone above high-weight. "Thanks, Bobo," Hugh said in parting. "Good eating." The dwarf grinned, ducked his head, and sped away, swarming up the ladder they had just descended.

Hugh turned and started down, touching his knife as he did so. It was good to feel it against him again. Not that it was his original knife. That had been Bobo's prize when he was captured, and Bobo had been unable to return it, having inadvertently left it sticking in a big one that got away. But the replacement Joe-Jim had given him was well balanced and quite satisfactory.

Bobo had conducted him, at Hugh's request and by Joe-Jim's order, down to the area directly over the auxiliary Converter used by the scientists. He wanted to find Bill Ertz, Assistant Chief Engineer and leader of the bloc of younger scientists, and he did not want to have to answer too many questions before he found him.

Hugh dropped quickly down the remaining levels and found himself in a main passageway which he recognized. Good! A turn to the left, a couple of hundred yards' walk and he found himself at the door of the compartment which housed the Converter. A guard lounged in front of it. Hugh started to push on past, was stopped. "Where do you think you're going?"

"I want to find Bill Ertz."

"You mean the Chief Engineer? Well, he's not here."

"Chief? What's happened to the old one?" Hoyland regretted the remark at once—but it was already out.

"Huh? The old Chief? Why, he's made the Trip long

since." The guard looked at him suspiciously. "What's wrong with you?"

"Nothing," denied Hugh. "Just a slip."

"Funny sort of a slip. Well, you'll find Chief Ertz around his office probably."

"Thanks. Good eating."

"Good eating."

Hugh was admitted to see Ertz after a short wait. Ertz looked up from his desk as Hugh came in. "Well," he said, "so you're back, and not dead after all. This *is* a surprise. We had written you off, you know, as making the Trip."

"Yes, I suppose so."

"Well, sit down and tell me about it—I've a little time to spare at the moment. Do you know, though, I wouldn't have recognized you. You've changed a lot—all that gray hair. I imagine you had some pretty tough times."

Gray hair? Was his hair gray? And Ertz had changed a lot, too, Hugh now noticed. He was paunchy and the lines in his face had set. Good Jordan! How long had he been gone?

Ertz drummed on his desk top, and pursed his lips. "It makes a problem—your coming back like this. I'm afraid I can't just assign you to your old job; Mort Tyler has that. But we'll find a place for you, suitable to your rank."

Hugh recalled Mort Tyler and not too favorably. A precious sort of a chap, always concerned with what was proper and according to regulations. So Tyler had actually made scientisthood, and was on Hugh's old job at the Converter. Well, it didn't matter. "That's all right," he began. "I wanted to talk to you about—"

"Of course, there's the matter of seniority," Ertz went on. "Perhaps the Council had better consider the matter. I don't know of a precedent. We've lost a number of scientists to the muties in the past, but you are the first to escape with his life in my memory."

"That doesn't matter," Hugh broke in. "I've something much more pressing to talk about. While I was away I found out some amazing things, Bill, things that it is of paramount importance for you to know about. That's why I came straight to you. Listen, I—"

Ertz was suddenly alert. "Of course you have! I must be slowing down. You must have had a marvelous opportunity to study the muties and scout out their territory. Come on, man, spill it! Give me your report."

Hugh wet his lips. "It's not what you think," he said. "It's much more important than just a report on the muties, though it concerns them, too. In fact, we may have to change our whole policy with respect to the mu—"

"Well, go ahead, go ahead! I'm listening."

"'All right." Hugh told him of his tremendous discovery as to the actual nature of the Ship, choosing his words carefully and trying very hard to be convincing. He dwelt lightly on the difficulties presented by an attempt to reorganize the Ship in accordance with the new concept and bore down heavily on the prestige and honor that would accrue to the man who led the effort.

He watched Ertz's face as he talked. After the first start of complete surprise when Hugh launched his key idea, the fact that the Ship was actually a moving body in a great outside space, his face became impassive and Hugh could read nothing in it, except that he seemed to detect a keener interest when Hugh spoke of how Ertz was just the man for the job because of his leadership of the younger, more progressive scientists.

When Hugh concluded, he waited for Ertz's response. Ertz said nothing at first, simply continued with his annoying habit of drumming on the top of his desk. Finally he said, "These are important matters, Hoyland, much too important to be dealt with casually. I must have time to chew it over."

"Yes, certainly," Hugh agreed. "I wanted to add that I've made arrangements for safe passage up to no-weight. I can take you up and let you see for yourself."

"No doubt that is best," Ertz replied. "Well—are you hungry?"

"No."

"Then we'll both sleep on it. You can use the compartment at the back of my office. I don't want you discussing this with anyone else until I've had time to think about it; it might cause unrest if it got out without proper preparation."

"Yes, you're right."

"Very well, then"—Ertz ushered him into a compartment behind his office which he very evidently used for a lounge—"have a good rest," he said, "and we'll talk later."

"Thanks," Hugh acknowledged. "Good eating."

"Good eating."

Once he was alone, Hugh's excitement gradually dropped away from him, and he realized that he was fagged out and very sleepy. He stretched out on a built-in couch and fell asleep.

When he awoke he discovered that the only door to the compartment was barred from the other side. Worse than that, his knife was gone.

He had waited an indefinitely long time when he heard activity at the door. It opened; two husky, unsmiling men entered. "Come along," said one of them. He sized them up, noting that neither of them carried a knife. No chance to snatch one from their belts, then. On the other hand he might be able to break away from them.

But beyond them, a wary distance away in the outer room, were two other equally formidable men, each armed with a knife. One balanced his for throwing; the other held his by the grip, ready to stab at close quarters.

He was boxed in and he knew it. They had anticipated his possible moves.

He had long since learned to relax before the inevitable. He composed his face and marched quietly out. Once through the door he saw Ertz, waiting and quite evidently in charge of the party of men. He spoke to him, being careful to keep his voice calm. "Hello, Bill. Pretty extensive preparations you've made. Some trouble, maybe?"

Ertz seemed momentarily uncertain of his answer, then said, "You're going before the Captain."

"Good!" Hugh answered. "Thanks, Bill. But do you think it's wise to try to sell the idea to him without laying a little preliminary foundation with the others?"

Ertz was annoyed at his apparent thickheadedness and showed it. "You don't get the idea," he growled. "You're going before the Captain to stand trial—for heresy!"

Hugh considered this as if the idea had not before occurred to him. He answered mildly, "You're off down the wrong passage, Bill. Perhaps a charge and trial is the best way to get at the matter, but I'm not a peasant, simply to be hustled before the Captain. I must be tried by the Council. I am a scientist."

"Are you now?" Ertz said softly. "I've had advice about that. You were written off the lists. Just what you are is a matter for the Captain to determine."

Hugh held his peace. It was against him, he could see, and there was no point in antagonizing Ertz. Ertz made a signal; the two unarmed men each grasped one of Hugh's arms. He went with them quietly.

Hugh looked at the Captain with new interest. The old man had not changed much—a little fatter, perhaps.

The Captain settled himself slowly down in his chair, and picked up the memorandum before him.

"What's this all about?" he began irritably. "I don't understand it."

Mort Tyler was there to present the case against Hugh, a circumstance which Hugh had had no way of anticipating and which added to his misgivings. He searched his boyhood recollections for some handle by which to reach the man's sympathy, found none. Tyler cleared his throat and commenced:

"This is the case of one Hugh Hoyland, Captain, formerly one of your junior scientists—"

"Scientist, eh? Why doesn't the Council deal with him?"

"Because he is no longer a scientist, Captain. He went over to the muties. He now returns among us, preaching heresy and seeking to undermine your authority."

The Captain looked at Hugh with the ready belligerency of a man jealous of his prerogatives.

"Is that so?" he bellowed. "What have you to say for yourself?"

"It is not true, Captain," Hugh answered. "All that I have said to anyone has been an affirmation of the absolute truth of our ancient knowledge. I have not disputed the truths under which we live; I have simply affirmed them more forcibly than is the ordinary custom I—"

"I still don't understand this," the Captain interrupted, shaking his head. "You're charged with heresy, yet you say you believe the Teachings. If you aren't guilty, why are you here?"

"Perhaps I can clear the matter up," put in Ertz. "Hoyland—"

"Well, I hope you can," the Captain went on. "Come —let's hear it."

Ertz proceeded to give a reasonably correct, but slanted, version of Hoyland's return and his strange story. The Captain listened, with an expression that varied between puzzlement and annoyance.

When Ertz had concluded, the Captain turned to Hugh. "Humph!" he said.

Hugh spoke immediately. "The gist of my contention, Captain, is that there is a place up at no-weight where you can actually *see* the truth of our faith that the Ship is moving, where you can actually see Jordan's Plan in operation. That is not a denial of faith; that affirms it. There is no need to take my word for it. Jordan Himself will prove it."

Seeing that the Captain appeared to be in a state of indecision, Tyler broke in: "Captain, there is a possible explanation of this incredible situation which I feel duty bound that you should hear. Offhand, there are two obvious interpretations of Hoyland's ridiculous story: He may simply be guilty of extreme heresy, or he may be a mutie at heart and engaged in a scheme to lure you into their hands. But there is a third, more charitable explanation and one which I feel within me is probably the true one.

"There is record that Hoyland was seriously considered for the Converter at his birth inspection, but that his deviation from normal was slight, being simply an overlarge head, and he was passed. It seems to me that the terrible experiences he has undergone at the hands of the muties have finally unhinged an unstable mind. The poor chap is simply not responsible for his own actions."

Hugh looked at Tyler with new respect. To absolve him of guilt and at the same time to make absolutely certain that Hugh would wind up making the Trip—how neat!

The Captain shook a palm at them. "This has gone on

long enough." Then, turning to Ertz: "Is there recommendation?"

"Yes, Captain. The Converter."

"Very well, then. I really don't see, Ertz," he continued testily, "why I should be bothered with these details. It seems to me that you should be able to handle discipline in your department without my help."

"Yes, Captain."

The Captain shoved back from his desk, started to get up. "Recommendation confirmed. Dismissed."

Anger flooded through Hugh at the unreasonable injustice of it. They had not even considered looking at the only real evidence he had in his defense. He heard a shout: "Wait!"—then discovered it was his own voice.

The Captain paused, looking at him.

"Wait a moment," Hugh went on, his words spilling out of their own accord. "This won't make any difference, for you're all so damn sure you know all the answers that you won't consider a fair offer to come see with your own eyes. Nevertheless— Nevertheless—it *still* moves!"

Hugh had plenty of time to think, lying in the compartment where they confined him to await the power needs of the Converter, time to think, and to second-guess his mistakes. Telling his tale to Ertz immediately—that had been mistake number one. He should have waited, become reacquainted with the man and felt him out, instead of depending on a friendship which had never been very close.

Second mistake, Mort Tyler. When he heard his name he should have investigated and found out just how much influence the man had with Ertz. He had known him of old, he should have known better.

Well, here he was, condemned as a mutant—or maybe as a heretic. It came to the same thing. He considered whether or not he should have tried to explain why mutants happened. He had learned about it himself in some of the old records in Joe-Jim's possession. No, it wouldn't wash. How could you explain about radiations from the Outside causing the birth of mutants when the listeners did not believe there was such a place as Outside? No, he had messed it up before he was ever taken before the Captain.

His self-recriminations were disturbed at last by the sound of his door being unfastened. It was too soon for another of the infrequent meals; he thought that they had come at last to take him away, and renewed his resolve to take someone with him.

But he was mistaken. He heard a voice of gentle dignity: "Son, son, how does this happen?" It was Lieutenant Nelson, his first teacher, looking older than ever and frail.

The interview was distressing for both of them. The old man, childless himself, had cherished great hopes for his protégé, even the ambition that he might eventually aspire to the captaincy, though he had kept his vicarious ambition to himself, believing it not good for the young to praise them too highly. It had hurt his heart when the youth was lost.

Now he had returned, a man, but under disgraceful conditions and under sentence of death.

The meeting was no less unhappy for Hugh. He had loved the old man, in his way, wanted to please him and needed his approval. But he could see, as he told his story, that Nelson was not capable of treating the the story as anything but an aberration of Hugh's mind, and he suspected that Nelson would rather see him meet a quick death in the Converter, his atoms smashed to hydrogen and giving up clean useful power, than have him live to make a mock of the ancient teachings.

In that he did the old man an injustice; he underrated Nelson's mercy, but not his devotion to "science." But let it be said for Hugh that, had there been no more at issue than his own personal welfare, he might have preferred death to breaking the heart of his benefactor—being a romantic and more than a bit foolish.

Presently the old man got up to leave, the visit having grown unendurable to each of them. "Is there anything I can do for you, son? Do they feed you well enough?"

"Quite well, thanks," Hugh lied.

"Is there anything else?"

"No—yes, you might send me some tobacco. I haven't had a chew in a long time."

"I'll take care of it. Is there anyone you would like to see?"

"Why, I was under the impression that I was not permitted visitors—ordinary visitors."

"You are right, but I think perhaps I may be able to get the rule relaxed. But you will have to give me your promise not to speak of your heresy," he added anxiously.

Hugh thought quickly. This was a new aspect, a new possibility. His uncle? No, while they had always got along well, their minds did not meet—they would greet each other as strangers. He had never made friends easily; Ertz had been his obvious next friend and now look at the damned thing! Then he recalled his village chum, Alan Mahoney, with whom he had played as a boy. True, he had seen practically nothing of him since the time he was apprenticed to Nelson. Still—

"Does Alan Mahoney still live in our village?"

"Why, yes."

"I'd like to see him, if he'll come."

Alan arrived, nervous, ill at ease, but plainly glad to see Hugh and very much upset to find him under sentence to make the Trip. Hugh pounded him on the back. "Good boy," he said. "I knew you would come."

"Of course, I would," protested Alan, "once I knew. But nobody in the village knew it. I don't think even the Witnesses knew it."

"Well, you're here, that's what matters. Tell me about yourself. Have you married?"

"Huh, uh, no. Let's not waste time talking about me. Nothing ever happens to me anyhow. How in Jordan's name did you get in this jam, Hugh?"

"I can't talk about that, Alan. I promised Lieutenant Nelson that I wouldn't."

"Well, what's a promise—*that* kind of a promise? You're in a *jam*, fellow."

"Don't I know it!"

"Somebody have it in for you?"

"Well—our old pal Mort Tyler didn't help any; I think I can say that much."

Alan whistled and nodded his head slowly. "That explains a lot."

"How come? You know something?"

"Maybe, maybe not. After you went away he married Edris Baxter."

"So? Hm-m-m—yes, that clears up a lot." He remained silent for a time.

Presently Alan spoke up: "Look, Hugh. You're not going to sit here and take it, are you? Particularly with Tyler mixed in it. We gotta get you outa here."

"How?"

"I don't know. Pull a raid, maybe. I guess I could get a few knives to rally round and help us—all good boys, spoiling for a fight."

"Then, when it's over, we'd all be for the Converter. You, me, and your pals. No, it won't wash."

"But we've *got* to do something. We can't just sit here and wait for them to burn you."

"I know that." Hugh studied Alan's face. Was it a fair thing to ask? He went on, reassured by what he had seen. "Listen. You would do anything you could to get me out of this, wouldn't you?"

"You know that." Alan's tone showed hurt.

"Very well, then. There is a dwarf named Bobo. I'll tell you how to find him—"

Alan climbed, up and up, higher than he had ever been since Hugh had led him, as a boy, into foolhardy peril. He was older now, more conservative; he had no stomach for it. To the very real danger of leaving the well-traveled lower levels was added his superstitious ignorance. But still he climbed.

This should be about the place—unless he had lost count. But he saw nothing of the dwarf.

Bobo saw him first. A slingshot load caught Alan in the pit of the stomach, even as he was shouting, "Bobo!"

Bobo backed into Joe-Jim's compartment and dumped his load at the feet of the twins. "Fresh meat," he said proudly.

"So it is," agreed Jim indifferently. "Well, it's yours; take it away."

The dwarf dug a thumb into a twisted ear, "Funny," he said, "he knows Bobo's name."

Joe looked up from the book he was reading—
Browning's *Collected Poems*, L-Press, New York, London,
Luna City, cr. 35. "That's interesting. Hold on a mo-
ment."

Hugh had prepared Alan for the shock of Joe-Jim's
appearance. In reasonably short order he collected
his wits sufficiently to be able to tell his tale. Joe-
Jim listened to it without much comment, Bobo with
interest but little comprehension.

When Alan concluded, Jim remarked, "Well, you
win, Joe. He didn't make it." Then, turning to Alan, he
added, "You can take Hoyland's place. Can you play
checkers?"

Alan looked from one head to the other. "But you
don't understand," he said. "Aren't you going to do
anything about it?"

Joe looked puzzled. "Us? Why should we?"

"But you've *got* to. Don't you see? He's depending on
you. There's nobody else he can look to. That's why I
came. Don't you see?"

"Wait a moment," drawled Jim, "wait a moment. Keep
your belt on. Supposing we did want to help him—which
we don't—how in Jordan's Ship could we? Answer me
that."

"Why—why—" Alan stumbled in the face of such
stupidity. "Why, get up a rescue party, of course, and go
down and get him out!"

"Why should we get ourselves killed in a fight to rescue
your friend?"

Bobo pricked his ears. "Fight?" he inquired eagerly.

"No, Bobo," Joe denied. "No fight. Just talk."

"Oh," said Bobo and returned to passivity.

Alan looked at the dwarf. "If you'd even let Bobo and
me—"

"No," Joe said shortly. "It's out of the question. Shut
up about it."

Alan sat in a corner, hugging his knees in despair. If
only he could get out of there. He could still try to stir
up some help down below. The dwarf seemed to be
asleep, though it was difficult to be sure with him. If only
Joe-Jim would sleep, too.

Joe-Jim showed no indication of sleepiness. Joe tried to continue reading, but Jim interrupted him from time to time. Alan could not hear what they were saying.

Presently Joe raised his voice. "Is that your idea of fun?" he demanded.

"Well," said Jim, "it beats checkers."

"It does, does it? Suppose you get a knife in your eye—where would I be then?"

"You're getting old, Joe. No juice in you any more."

"You're as old as I am."

"Yeah, but I got young ideas."

"Oh, you make me sick. Have it your own way—but don't blame me. Bobo!"

The dwarf sprang up at once, alert. "Yeah, Boss."

"Go out and dig up Squatty and Long Arm and Pig." Joe-Jim got up, went to a locker, and started pulling knives out of their racks.

Hugh heard the commotion in the passageway outside his prison. It could be the guards coming to take him to the Converter, though they probably wouldn't be so noisy. Or it could be just some excitement unrelated to him. On the other hand it might be—

It was. The door burst open, and Alan was inside, shouting at him and thrusting a brace of knives into his hands. He was hurried out of the door, while stuffing the knives in his belt and accepting two more.

Outside he saw Joe-Jim, who did not see him at once, as he was methodically letting fly, as calmly as if he had been engaging in target practice in his own study. And Bobo, who ducked his head and grinned with a mouth widened by a bleeding cut, but continued the easy flow of the motion whereby he loaded and let fly. There were three others, two of whom Hugh recognized as belonging to Joe-Jim's privately owned gang of bullies—muties by definition and birthplace; they were not deformed.

The count does not include still forms on the floor plates.

"Come on!" yelled Alan. "There'll be more in no time." He hurried down the passage to the right.

Joe-Jim desisted and followed him. Hugh let one blade go for luck at a figure running away to the left. The target

as poor, and he had no time to see if he had drawn blood.
They scrambled along the passage, Bobo bringing up the
rear, as if reluctant to leave the fun, and came to a point
where a side passage crossed the main one.

Alan led them to the right again. "Stairs ahead," he
shouted.

They did not reach them. An airtight door, rarely used,
clanged in their faces ten yards short of the stairs. Joe-Jim's
bravoes checked their flight and they looked doubtfully
at their master. Bobo broke his thickened nails trying to
get a purchase on the door.

The sounds of pursuit were clear behind them.

"Boxed in," said Joe softly. "I hope you like it, Jim."

Hugh saw a head appear around the corner of the passage they had quitted. He threw overhand but the distance
was too great; the knife clanged harmlessly against steel.
The head disappeared. Long Arm kept his eye on the
spot, his sling loaded and ready.

Hugh grabbed Bobo's shoulder. "Listen! Do you see
that light?"

The dwarf blinked stupidly. Hugh pointed to the intersection of the glowtubes where they crossed in the overhead
directly above the junction of the passages. "That light.
Can you hit them where they cross?"

Bobo measured the distance with his eye. It would be
hard shot under any conditions at that range. Here, con-
stricted as he was by the low passageway, it called for
fast, flat trajectory, and allowance for higher weight
than he was used to.

He did not answer. Hugh felt the wind of his swing but
did not see the shot. There was a tinkling crash; the passage became dark.

"Now!" yelled Hugh, and led them away at a run. As
they neared the intersection he shouted, "Hold your breaths!
Mind the gas!" The radioactive vapor poured lazily out
from the broken tube above and filled the crossing with
greenish mist.

Hugh ran to the right, thankful for his knowledge as
an engineer of the lighting circuits. He had picked the
right direction; the passage ahead was black, being ser-
viced from beyond the break. He could hear footsteps

around him; whether they were friend or enemy he di
not know.

They burst into light. No one was in sight but a scare
and harmless peasant who scurried away at an unlike
pace. They took a quick muster. All were present, b
Bobo was making heavy going of it.

Joe looked at him. "He sniffed the gas, I think. Poun
his back."

Pig did so with a will. Bobo belched deeply, wa
suddenly sick, then grinned.

"He'll do," decided Joe.

The slight delay had enabled one at least to catc
up with them. He came plunging out of the dark
unaware of, or careless of, the strength against him
Alan knocked Pig's arm down, as he raised it to throw.

"Let me at 'im!" he demanded. "He's mine!"

It was Tyler.

"Man-fight?" Alan challenged, thumb on his blade.

Tyler's eyes darted from adversary to adversary an
accepted the invitation to individual duel by lunging a
Alan. The quarters were too cramped for throwing; the
closed, each achieving his grab in parry, fist to wrist.

Alan was stockier, probably stronger; Tyler was slip
pery. He attempted to give Alan a knee to the crotch
Alan evaded it, stamped on Tyler's planted foot. The
went down. There was a crunching crack.

A moment later, Alan was wiping his knife agains
his thigh. "Let's get goin'," he complained. "I'm scared."

They reached a stairway, and raced up it, Long Arn
and Pig ahead to fan out on each level and cover thei
flanks, and the third of the three choppers—Hugh hear
him called Squatty—covering the rear. The others bunche
in between.

Hugh thought they had won free, when he hear
shouts and the clatter of a thrown knife just above him
He reached the level above in time to be cut not dee
ly but jaggedly by a ricocheted blade.

Three men were down. Long Arm had a blade stickin
in the fleshy part of his upper arm, but it did no
seem to bother him. His slingshot was still spinning. Pi
was scrambling after a thrown knife, his own armamen
exhausted. But there were signs of his work; one man wa

down on one knee some twenty feet away. He was bleeding from a knife wound in the thigh.

As the figure steadied himself with one hand against the bulkhead and reached toward an empty belt with the other, Hugh recognized him.

Bill Ertz.

He had led a party up another way and flanked them, to his own ruin. Bobo crowded behind Hugh and got his mighty arm free for the cast. Hugh caught at it. "Easy, Bobo," he directed. "In the stomach, and easy."

The dwarf looked puzzled, but did as he was told. Ertz folded over at the middle and slid to the deck.

"Well placed," said Jim.

"Bring him along, Bobo," directed Hugh, "and stay in the middle." He ran his eye over their party, now huddled at the top of that flight of stairs. "All right, gang— up we go again! Watch it."

Long Arm and Pig swarmed up the next flight, the others disposing themselves as usual. Joe looked annoyed. In some fashion—a fashion by no means clear at the moment—he had been eased out as leader of this gang—*his* gang—and Hugh was giving orders. He reflected that there was no time now to make a fuss. It might get them all killed.

Jim did not appear to mind. In fact, he seemed to be enjoying himself.

They put ten more levels behind them with no organized opposition. Hugh directed them not to kill peasants unnecessarily. The three bravoes obeyed; Bobo was too loaded down with Ertz to constitute a problem in discipline. Hugh saw to it that they put thirty-odd more decks below them and were well into no man's land before he let vigilance relax at all. Then he called a halt and they examined wounds.

The only deep ones were to Long Arm's arm and Bobo's face. Joe-Jim examined them and applied presses with which he had outfitted himself before starting. Hugh refused treatment for his flesh wound. "It's stopped bleeding," he insisted, "and I've got a lot to do."

"You've got nothing to do but to get up home," said J "and that will be an end to this foolishness."

"Not quite," denied Hugh. "You may be going home,

but Alan and I and Bobo are going up to no-weight—to the Captain's veranda."

"Nonsense," said Joe. "What for?"

"Come along if you like, and see. All right, gang. Let's go."

Joe started to speak, stopped when Jim kept still. Joe-Jim followed along.

They floated gently through the door of the veranda, Hugh, Alan, Bobo with his still-passive burden—and Joe-Jim. "That's it," said Hugh to Alan, waving his hand at the splendid stars, "that's what I've been telling you about."

Alan looked and clutched at Hugh's arm. "Jordan!" he moaned. "We'll fall out!" He closed his eyes tightly.

Hugh shook him. "It's all right," he said. "It's grand. Open your eyes."

Joe-Jim touched Hugh's arm. "What's it all about?" he demanded. "Why did you bring *him* up here?" He pointed to Ertz.

"Oh—him. Well, when he wakes up I'm going to show him the stars, prove to him that the Ship moves."

"Well? What for?"

"Then I'll send him back down to convince some others."

"Hm-m-m—suppose he doesn't have any better luck than you had?"

"Why, then"—Hugh shrugged his shoulders—"why, then we shall just have to do it all over, I suppose, till we do convince them.

"We've got to do it, you know."

Part Two

COMMON SENSE

II

COMMON SENSE

JOE, THE RIGHT HAND head of Joe-Jim, addressed his words to Hugh Hoyland. "All right, smart boy, you've convinced the Chief Engineer—" He gestured toward Bill Ertz with the blade of his knife, then resumed picking Jim's teeth with it. "So what? Where does it get you?"

"I've explained that," Hugh Hoyland answered irritably. "We keep on, until every scientist in the Ship, from the Captain to the greenest probationer, *knows* that the Ship moves and believes that we can make it move. Then we'll finish the Trip, as Jordan willed. How many knives can you muster?" he added.

"Well, for the love o' Jordan! Listen—have you got some fool idea that we are going to *help* you with this crazy scheme?"

"Naturally. You're necessary to it."

"Then you had better think up another think. That's out. Bobo! Get out the checkerboard."

"O.K., Boss." The microcephalic dwarf hunched himself up off the floor plates and trotted across Joe-Jim's apartment.

"Hold it, Bobo." Jim, the left-hand head, had spoken. The dwarf stopped dead, his narrow forehead wrinkled. The fact that his two-headed master occasionally failed to agree as to what Bobo should do was the only note of insecurity in his tranquil bloodthirsty existence.

"Let's hear what he has to say," Jim continued. "There may be some fun in this."

"Fun! The fun of getting a knife in your ribs. Let me point out that they are my ribs, too. I don't agree to it."

"I didn't ask you to agree; I asked you to listen. Leaving fun out of it, it may be the only way to keep a knife out of our ribs."

"What do you mean?" Joe demanded suspiciously.

"You heard what Ertz had to say." Jim flicked a thumb toward the prisoner. "The Ship's officers are planning to clean out the upper levels. How would you like to go into the Converter, Joe? You can't play checkers after we're broken down into hydrogen."

"Bunk! The Crew can't exterminate the muties—they've tried before."

Jim turned to Ertz. "How about it?"

Ertz answered somewhat diffidently, being acutely aware of his own changed status from a senior Ship's officer to prisoner of war. He felt befuddled anyhow; too much had happened and too fast. He had been kidnaped, hauled up to the Captain's veranda, and had there gazed out at the stars—the *stars*.

His hard-boiled rationalism included no such concept. If an Earth astronomer had had it physically demonstrated to him that the globe spun on its axis because someone turned a crank, the upset in evaluations could have been no greater.

Besides that, he was acutely aware that his own continued existence hung in fine balance. Joe-Jim was the first upper-level mutie he had ever met other than in combat, knife to knife. A word from him to that great ugly dwarf sprawled on the deck—

He chose his words. "I think the Crew would be successful, this time. We . . . they have organized for it. Unless there are more of you than we think there are and better organized, I think it could be done. You see . . . well, uh, I organized it."

"You?"

"Yes. A good many of the Council don't like the policy of letting the muties alone. Maybe it's sound religious doctrine and maybe it isn't, but we lose a child here and a couple of pigs there. It's annoying."

"What do you expect muties to eat?" demanded Jim belligerently. "Thin air?"

"No, not exactly. Anyhow, the new policy was not entirely destructive. Any muties that surrendered and could be civilized we planned to give to masters and put them to work as part of the Crew. That is, any that weren't, uh . . . that were—" He broke off in embarrassment, and shifted his eyes from the two-headed monstrosity before him.

"You mean any that weren't physical mutations, like me," Joe filled in nastily. "Don't you?" he persisted. "For the likes of me it's the Converter, isn't it?" He slapped the blade of his knife nervously on the palm of his hand.

Ertz edged away, his own hand shifting to his belt. But no knife was slung there; he felt naked and helpless without it. "Just a minute," he said defensively, "you asked me; that's the situation. It's out of my hands. I'm just telling you."

"Let him alone, Joe. He's just handing you the straight dope. It's like I was telling you—either go along with Hugh's plan, or wait to be hunted down. And don't get any ideas about killing him—we're going to need him." As Jim spoke he attempted to return the knife to its sheath. There was a brief and silent struggle between the twins for control of the motor nerves to their right arm, a clash of will below the level of physical activity. Joe gave in.

"All right," he agreed surlily, "but if I go to the Converter, I want to take this one with me for company."

"Stow it," said Jim. "You'll have me for company."

"Why do you believe him?"

"He has nothing to gain by lying. Ask Alan."

Alan Mahoney, Hugh's friend and boyhood chum, had listened to the argument round-eyed, without joining it. He, too, had suffered the nerve-shaking experience of viewing the outer stars, but his ignorant peasant mind had not the sharply formulated opinions of Ertz, the Chief Engineer. Ertz had been able to see almost at once that the very existence of a world outside the Ship changed all his plans and everything he had believed in; Alan was capable only of wonder.

"What about this plan to fight the muties, Alan?"

"Huh? Why, I don't know anything about it. Shucks, I'm not a scientist. Say, wait a minute—there was a junior officer sent in to help our village scientist, Lieutenant Nelson—" He stopped and looked puzzled.

"What about it? Go ahead."

"Well, he has been organizing the cadets in our village, and the married men, too, but not so much. Making 'em practice with their blades and slings. Never told us what for, though."

Ertz spread his hands. "You see?"

Joe nodded. "I see," he admitted grimly.

Hugh Hoyland looked at him eagerly. "Then you're with me?"

"I suppose so," Joe admitted. "Right!" added Jim.

Hoyland looked back to Ertz. "How about you, Bill Ertz?"

"What choice have I got?"

"Plenty. I want you with me wholeheartedly. Here's the layout: The Crew doesn't count; it's the officers we have to convince. Any that aren't too addlepated and stiff-necked to understand after they've seen the stars and the Control Room, we keep. The others" —he drew a thumb across his throat while making a harsh sibilance in his cheek—"the Converter."

Bobo grinned happily and imitated the gesture and the sound.

Ertz nodded. "Then what?"

"Muties and Crew together, under a new Captain, we move the Ship to Far Centaurus! Jordan's Will be done!"

Ertz stood up and faced Hoyland. It was a heady notion, too big to be grasped at once, but, by Jordan! he liked it. He spread his hands on the table and leaned across it. "I'm with you, Hugh Hoyland!"

A knife clattered on the table before him, one from the brace at Joe-Jim's belt. Joe looked startled, seemed about to speak to his brother, then appeared to think better of it. Ertz looked his thanks and stuck the knife in his belt.

The twins whispered to each other for a moment, then Joe spoke up. "Might as well make it stick," he said. He drew his remaining knife and, grasping the blade between thumb and forefinger so that only the point was exposed, he jabbed himself in the fleshly upper part of his left arm. "Blade for blade!"

Ertz's eyebrows shot up. He whipped out his newly acquired blade and cut himself in the same location. The blood spurted and ran down to the crook of his arm. "Back to back!" He shoved the table aside and pressed his gory shoulder against the wound on Joe-Jim.

Alan Mahoney, Hugh Hoyland, Bobo—all had their blades out, all nicked their arms till the skin ran red and wet. They crowded in, bleeding shoulders pushed together so that the blood dripped united to the deck.

"Blade for blade!"

"Back to back!"

"Blood to blood!"

"Blood brothers—*to the end of the Trip!*"

An apostate scientist, a kidnaped scientist, a dull peasant, a two-headed monster, a apple-brained moron—five knives, counting Joe-Jim as one; five brains, counting Joe-Jim as two and Bobo as none—five brains and five knives to overthrow an entire culture.

"But I don't want to go back, Hugh." Alan shuffled his feet and looked dogged. "Why can't I stay here with you? I'm a good blade."

"Sure you are, old fellow. But right now you'll be more useful as a spy."

"But you've got Bill Ertz for that."

"So we have, but we need you too. Bill is a public figure; he can't duck out and climb to the upper levels without it being noticed and causing talk. That's where you come in—you're his go-between."

"I'll have a Huff of a time explaining where I've been."

"Don't explain any more than you have to. But stay away from the Witness." Hugh had a sudden picture of Alan trying to deceive the old village historian, with his searching tongue and lust for details. "Keep clear of the Witness. The old boy would trip you up."

"Him? You mean the old one—he's dead. Made the Trip long since. The new one don't amount to nothing."

"Good. If you're careful, you'll be safe." Hugh raised his voice. "Bill! Are you ready to go down?"

"I suppose so." Ertz picked himself up and reluctantly put aside the book he had been reading—*The Three Musketeers*, illustrated, one of Joe-Jim's carefully stolen library. "Say, that's a wonderful book. Hugh, is *Earth* really like that?"

"Of course. Doesn't it say so in the book?"

Ertz chewed his lip and thought about it. "What is a house?"

"A house? A house is a sort of a . . . a sort of a compartment."

"That's what I thought at first, but how can you ride on a compartment?"

"Huh? What do you mean?"

"Why, all through the book they keep climbing on their houses and riding away."

"Let me see that book," Joe ordered. Ertz handed it to him. Joe-Jim thumbed through it rapidly. "I see what you mean. Idiot! They ride horses, not houses."

"Well, what's a horse?"

"A horse is an animal, like a big hog, or maybe like a cow. You squat up on top of it and let it carry you along."

Ertz considered this. "It doesn't seem practical. Look—when you ride in a litter, you tell the chief porter where you want to go. How can you tell a cow where you want to go?"

"That's easy. You have a porter lead it."

Ertz conceded the point. "Anyhow, you might fall off. It isn't practical. I'd rather walk."

"It's quite a trick," Joe explained. "Takes practice."

"Can *you* do it?"

Jim sniggered. Joe looked annoyed. "There are no horses in the Ship."

"O.K., O.K. But look— These guys Athos, Porthos, and Aramis, they had something—"

"We can discuss that later," Hugh interrupted. "Bobo is back. Are you ready to go, Bill?"

"Don't get in a hurry, Hugh. This is important. These chaps had knives——"

"Sure. Why not?"

"But they were better than our knives. They had knives as long as your arm——maybe longer. If we are going to fight the whole Crew, think what an advantage that would be."

"Hm-m-m——" Hugh drew his knife and looked at it, cradling it in his palm. "Maybe. You couldn't throw it as well."

"We could have throwing knives, too."

"Yes, I suppose we could."

The twins had listened without comment. "He's right," put in Joe. "Hugh, you take care of placing the knives. Jim and I have some reading to do." Both of Joe-Jim's heads were busy thinking of other books they owned, books that discussed in saguinary detail the infinitely varied methods used by mankind to shorten the lives of enemies. He was about to institute a War College Department of Historical Research, although he called his project by no such fancy term.

"O.K.," Hugh agreed, "but you will have to say the word to them."

"Right away." Joe-Jim stepped out of his apartment into the passageway where Bobo had assembled a couple of dozen of Joe-Jim's henchmen among the muties. Save for Long Arm, Pig, and Squatty, who had taken part in the rescue of Hugh, they were all strangers to Hugh, Alan, and Bill——and they were all sudden death to strangers.

Joe-Jim motioned for the three from the lower decks to join him. He pointed them out to the muties, and ordered them to look closely and not to forget——these three were to have safe passage and protection wherever they went. Furthermore, in Joe-Jim's absence his men were to take orders from any of them.

They stirred and looked at each other. Orders they were used to, but from Joe-Jim only.

A big-nosed individual rose up from his squat and addressed them. He looked at Joe-Jim, but his words were intended for all. "I am Jack-of-the-Nose. My blade is sharp and my eye is keen. Joe-Jim with the two wise heads is my Boss and my knife fights for him. But Joe-Jim is my Boss, not strangers from heavy decks. What do you say, knives? Is that not the Rule?"

He paused. The others had listened to him nervously, stealing glances at Joe-Jim. Joe muttered something out of the corner of his mouth to Bobo. Jack O'Nose opened his mouth to continue. There was a smash of breaking teeth, a crack from a broken neck; his mouth was stopped with a missile

Bobo reloaded his slingshot. The body, not yet dead, settled slowly to the deck. Joe-Jim waved a hand toward it. "Good eating!" Joe announced. "He's yours." The muties converged on the body as if they had suddenly been unleashed. They concealed it completely in a busy grunting pile-up. Knives out, they cuffed and crowded each other for a piece of the prize.

Joe-Jim waited patiently for the undoing to be finished, then, when the place where Jack O'Nose had been was no more than a stain on the deck and the several private arguments over the sharing had died down, he spoke again—Joe spoke. "Long Arm, you and Forty-one and the Ax go down with Bobo, Alan and Bill. The rest wait here."

Bobo trotted away in the long loping strides permitted by the low pseudogravity near the axis of rotation of the Ship. Three of the muties detached themselves from the pack and followed. Ertz and Alan Mahoney hurried to catch up.

When he reached the nearest staircase trunk, Bobo skipped out into space without breaking his stride and let centrifugal force carry him down to the next deck. Alan and the muties followed, but Ertz paused at the edge and looked back. "Jordan keep you, brothers!" he sang out.

Joe-Jim waved to him. "And you," acknowledged Joe.

"Good eating!" Jim added.

"Good eating!"

Bobo led them down forty-odd decks, well into the no man's land inhabited neither by mutie nor crew, and stopped. He pointed in succession to Long Arm, Forty-one, and the Ax. "Two Wise Heads say for you to keep watch here. You first," he added, pointing again to Forty-one.

"It's like this," Ertz amplified. "Alan and I are going down to heavy-weight level. You three are to keep a guard here, one at a time, so that I will be able to send messages back up to Joe-Jim. Get it?"

"Sure. Why not?" Long Arm answered.

"Joe-Jim says it," Forty-one commented with a note of finality in his voice. The Ax grunted agreeably.

"O.K.," said Bobo. Forty-one sat down at the stairwell, letting his feet hang over, and turned his attention to food which he had been carrying tucked under his left arm.

Bobo slapped Ertz and Alan on their backs. "Good eating," he bade them, grinning. When he could get his breath, Ertz acknowledged the courteous thought, then dropped at once to the next lower deck, Alan close after him. They had still many decks to go to "civilization."

Commander Phineas Narby, Executive Assistant to Jordan's Captain, in rummaging through the desk of the Chief Engineer was amused to find that Bill Ertz had secreted therein a couple of Unnecessary books. There were the usual Sacred books, of course, including the priceless *Care and Maintenance of the Auxiliary Four-stage Converter* and the *Handbook of Power, Light, and Conditioning—Starship* Vanguard. These were Sacred books of the first order, bearing the imprint of Jordan himself, and could lawfully be held only by the Chief Engineer.

Narby considered himself a skeptic and rationalist. Belief in Jordan was a good thing—for the Crew. Nevertheless the sight of a title page with the words "Jordan Foundation" on it stirred up within him a trace of religious awe such as he had not felt since before he was admitted to scientisthood.

He knew that the feeling was irrational—probably there had been at some time in the past some person or persons called Jordan. Jordan might have been an early engineer or captain who codified the common sense and almost instinctive rules for running the Ship. Or, as seemed more likely, the Jordan myth went back much farther than this book in his hand, and its author had simply availed himself of the ignorant superstitions of the Crew to give his writings authority. Narby knew how such things were done—he planned to give the new policy with respect to the muties the same blessing of Jordan when the time was ripe for it to be put into execution. Yes, order and discipline and belief in authority were good things—for the Crew. It was equally evident that a rational, coolheaded common sense was a proper attribute for the scientists who were custodians of the Ship's welfare—common sense and a belief in nothing but facts.

He admired the exact lettering on the pages of the book he held. They certainly had excellent clerks in those ancient times—not the sloppy draftsmen he was forced to put up with, who could hardly print two letters alike.

He made a mental note to study these two indispensable handbooks of the engineering department before turning them over to Ertz's successor. It would be well, he thought, not to be too dependent on the statements of the Chief Engineer when he himself succeeded to the captaincy. Narby had no particular respect for engineers, largely because he had no particular talent for engineering. When he had first reached scientisthood and had been charged to defend the spiritual and material welfare of the Crew, had sworn to uphold the Teachings of Jordan, he soon discovered that administration and personnel management were more in his lines than tending the converter or servicing the power lines. He had served as clerk, village administrator, recorder to the Council, personnel officer, and was now chief executive for Jordan's Captain himself—ever since an unfortunate and rather mysterious accident had shortened the life of Narby's predecessor in that post.

His decision to study up on engineering before a new Chief Engineer was selected brought to mind the problem of choosing a new chief. Normally the Senior Watch Officer for the Converter would become Chief Engineer when a chief made the Trip, but in this case, Mort Tyler, the Senior Watch, had made the Trip at the same time—his body had been found, stiff and cold, after the mutie raid which had rescued the heretic, Hugh Hoyland. That left the choice wide open and Narby was a bit undecided as to whom he should suggest to the Captain.

One thing was certain—the new chief must not be a man with as much aggressive initiative as Ertz. Narby admitted that Ertz had done a good job in organizing the Crew for the proposed extermination of the muties, but his very efficiency had made him too strong a candidate for succession to the captaincy—if and when. Had he thought about it overtly Narby might have admitted to himself that the present Captain's life span had extended unduly because Narby was not absolutely certain that Ertz would not be selected.

What he did think was that this might be a good time for the old Captain to surrender his spirit to Jordan. The fat old fool had long outlived his usefulness; Narby was tired of having to wheedle him into giving the proper orders. If the Council were faced with the necessity of selecting a new Captain at this time, there was but one candidate available—

Narby put the book down, his mind made up.

The simple decision to eliminate the old Captain carried with it in Narby's mind no feeling of shame, nor sin, nor disloyalty. He felt contempt but not dislike for the Captain, and no mean spirit colored his decision to kill him. Narby's plans were made on the noble level of statesmanship. He honestly believed that his objective was the welfare of the entire Crew—common-sense administration, order and discipline, good eating for everyone. He selected himself because it was obvious to him that he was best fitted to accomplish those worthy ends. That some must make the Trip in order that these larger interests be served he did not find even mildly regrettable, but he bore them no malice.

"What in the Huff are you doing at my desk?"

Narby looked up to see the late Bill Ertz standing over him, not looking pleased. He looked again, then as an afterthought closed his mouth. He had been so certain, when Ertz failed to reappear after the raid, that he had made the Trip and was in all probability butchered and eaten—so certain that it was now a sharp wrench to his mind to see Ertz standing before him, aggressively alive. But he pulled himself together.

"Bill! Jordan bless you, man—we thought you had made the Trip! Sit down, sit down, and tell me what happened to you."

"I will if you will get out of my chair," Ertz answered bitingly.

"Oh—sorry!" Narby hastily vacated the chair at Ertz's desk and found another.

"And now," Ertz continued, taking the seat Narby had left, "you might explain why you were going through my writings."

Narby managed to look hurt. "Isn't that obvious? We assumed you were dead. Someone had to take over and attend to your department until a new chief was designated. I was acting on behalf of the Captain."

Ertz looked him in the eyes. "Don't give me that guff, Narby. You know and I know who puts words in the Captain's mouth—we've planned it often enough. Even if you did think I was dead, it seems to me you could wait longer than the time between two sleeps to pry through my desk."

"Now really, old man—when a person is missing after a mutie raid, it's a common-sense assumption that he has made the Trip."

"O.K., O.K., skip it. Why didn't Mort Tyler take over in the meantime?"

"He's in the Converter."

"Killed, eh? But who ordered him put in the Converter? That much mass will make a terrific peak in the load."

"I did, in place of Hugh Hoyland. Their masses were nearly the same, and your requisition for the mass of Hugh Hoyland was unfilled."

"Nearly the same isn't good enough in handling the Converter. I'll have to check on it." He started to rise.

"Don't get excited," said Narby. "I'm not an utter fool in engineering, you know. I ordered his mass to be trimmed according to the same schedule you had laid out for Hoyland."

"Well—all right. That will do for now. But I will have to check it. We can't afford to waste mass."

"Speaking of waste mass," Narby said sweetly, "I found a couple of Unnecessary books in your desk."

"Well?"

"They are classed as mass available for power, you know."

"So? And who is the custodian of mass allocated for power?"

"You are certainly. But what were they doing in your desk?"

"Let me point out to you, my dear Captain's Best Boy, that it lies entirely within my discretion where I choose to store mass available for power."

"Hm-m-m—I suppose you are right. By the way, if you don't need them for the power schedule at once, would you mind letting me read them?"

"Not at all, if you want to be reasonable about it. I'll check them out to you—have to do that; they've already been centrifuged. Just be discreet about it."

"Thanks. Some of those ancients had vivid imaginations. Utterly crazy, of course, but amusing for relaxation."

Ertz got out the two volumes and prepared a receipt for Narby to sign. He did this absent-mindedly, being preoccupied with the problem of how and when to tackle Narby. Phineas Narby he knew to be a key man in the task he and his blood brothers had undertaken—perhaps *the* key man. If he could be won over—

"Fin," he said, when Narby had signed, "I wonder if we followed the wisest policy in Hoyland's case."

Narby looked surprised, but said nothing.

"Oh, I don't mean that I put any stock in his story," Ertz added hastily, "but I feel that we missed an opportunity. We should have kidded him along. He was a contact with the muties. The worst handicap we work under in trying to bring mutie country under the rule of the Council is the fact that we know very little about them. We don't know how many of them there are, nor how strong they are, or how well organized. Besides that, we will have to carry the fight to them and that's a big disadvantage. We don't really know our way around the upper decks. If we had played along with him and pretended to believe his story, we might have learned a lot of things."

"But we couldn't rely on what he told us," Narby pointed out.

"We didn't need to. He offered us an opportunity to go all the way to no-weight, and look around."

Narby looked astounded. "You surely aren't serious? A member of the Crew that trusted the muties' promise not to harm him wouldn't get up to no-weight; he'd make the Trip—fast!"

"I'm not so certain about that," Ertz objected. "Hoyland believed his own story—I'm sure of that; And—"

"What! All that utter nonsense about the Ship being capable of *moving*. The solid Ship." He pounded the bulkhead. "No one could believe that."

"But I tell you he did. He's a religious fanatic—granted. But he saw something up there, and that was how he interpreted it. We could have gone up to see whatever it was he was raving about and used the chance to scout out the muties."

"Utterly foolhardy!"

"I don't think so. He must have a great deal of influence among the muties; look at the trouble they went to just to rescue him. If he says he can give us safe passage up to no-weight, I think he can."

"Why this sudden change of opinion?"

"It was the raid that changed my mind. If anyone had told me that a gang of muties would come clear down to high-weight and risk their necks to save the life of one man I would not have believed him. But it happened. I'm forced to revise my opinions. Quite aside from his story, it's evident that the muties will fight for him and probably take orders from him. If that is true, it would be worth while to pander to his religious convictions if it would enable us to gain control over the muties without having to fight for it."

Narby shrugged it off. "Theoretically you may have something there. But why waste time over might-have-beens? If there was such an opportunity, we missed it."

"Maybe not. Hoyland is still alive and back with the muties. If I could figure out some way of getting a message to him, we might still be able to arrange it."

"But how could you?"

"I don't know exactly. I might take a couple of the boys and do some climbing. If we could capture a mutie without killing him, it might work out."

"A slim chance."

"I'm willing to risk it."

Narby turned the matter over in his mind. The whole plan seemed to him to be filled with long chances and foolish assumptions. Nevertheless if Ertz were willing to take the risk and it *did* work, Narby's dearest ambition would be much nearer realization. Subduing the muties by force would be a long and bloody job, perhaps an impossible job. He was clearly aware of its difficulty.

If it did not work, nothing was lost—but Ertz. Now that he thought it over, Ertz would be no loss at this point in the game. Hm-m-m.

"Go ahead," he said. "You are a brave man, but it's a worth-while venture."

"O.K.," Ertz agreed. "Good eating."

Narby took the hint. "Good eating," he answered, gathered up the books, and left. It did not occur to him until later that Ertz had not told him where he had been for so long.

And Ertz was aware that Narby had not been entirely frank with him, but, knowing Narby, he was not surprised. He was pleased enough that his extemporaneous groundwork for future action had been so well received. It never did occur to him that it might have been simpler and more effective to tell the truth.

Ertz busied himself for a short time in making a routine inspection of the Converter and appointed an acting Senior Watch Officer. Satisfied that his department could then take care of itself during a further absence, he sent for his chief porter and told the servant to fetch Alan Mahoney from his village. He had considered ordering his litter and meeting Mahoney halfway, but he decided against it as being too conspicuous.

Alan greeted him with enthusiasm. To him, still an unmarried cadet and working for more provident men when his contemporaries were all heads of families and solid men of property, the knowledge that he was blood brother to a senior scientist was quite the most important thing that had ever happened to him, even overshadowing his recent adventures, the meaning of which he was hardly qualified to understand anyway.

Ertz cut him short, and hastily closed the door to the outer engineering office. "Walls have ears," he said quietly, "and certainly clerks have ears, and tongues as well. Do you want us both to make the Trip?"

"Aw, gosh, Bill . . . I didn't mean to—"

"Never mind. I'll meet you on the same stair trunk we came down by, ten decks above this one. Can you count?"

"Sure, I can count that much. I can count twice that much. One and one makes two, and one more makes three, and one more makes four, and one makes five, and—"

"That's enough. I see you can. But I'm relying more on your loyalty and your knife than I am on your mathematical ability. Meet me there as soon as you can. Go up somewhere where you won't be noticed."

Forty-one was still on watch when they reached the rendezvous. Ertz called him by name while standing out of range of slingshot or thrown knife, a reasonable precaution in dealing with a creature who had grown to man size by being fast with his weapons. Once identification had been established, he directed the guard to find Hugh Hoyland. He and Alan sat down to wait.

Forty-one failed to find Hugh Hoyland at Joe-Jim's apartment. Nor was Joe-Jim there. He did find Bobo, but the pinhead was not very helpful. Hugh, Bobo told him, had gone up where-everybody-flies. That meant very little to Forty-one; he had been up to no-weight only once in his life. Since the level of weightlessness extended the entire length of the Ship, being in fact the last concentric cylinder around the Ship's axis—not that Forty-one could conceive it in those terms—the information that Hugh had headed for no-weight was not helpful.

Forty-one was puzzled. An order from Joe-Jim was not to be ignored and he had got it through his not overbright mind that an order from Ertz carried the same weight. He woke Bobo up again. "Where is the Two Wise Heads?"

"Gone to see knifemaker." Bobo closed his eyes again.

That was better. Forty-one knew where the knifemaker lived. Every mutie had dealings with her; she was the indispensable artisan and tradesman of mutie country. Her person was necessarily taboo; her workshop and the adjacent neighborhood were neutral territory for all. He scurried up two decks and hurried thence.

A door reading THERMODYNAMIC LABORA-TORY—KEEP OUT was standing open. Forty-one could not read; neither the name nor the injunction mattered to him. But he could hear voices, one of which he identified as coming from the twins, the other from the knifemaker. He walked in. "Boss—" he began.

"Shut up," said Joe. Jim did not look around but continued his argument with the Mother of Blades. "You'll make knives," he said, "and none of your lip."

She faced him, her four calloused hands set firmly on her broad hips. Her eyes were reddened from staring into the furnace in which she heated her metal; sweat ran down her wrinkled face into the sparse gray mustache which disfigured her upper lip, and dripped onto her bare chest. "Sure I make knives," she snapped. "Honest knives. Not pig-stickers like you want me to make. Knives as long as your arm—*ptui!*" She spat at the cherry-red lip of the furnace.

"Listen, you old Crew bait," Jim replied evenly, "you'll make knives the way I tell you to, or I'll toast your feet in your own furnace. Hear me?"

Forty-one was struck speechless. No one *ever* talked back to the Mother of Blades; the Boss was certainly a man of power!

The knifemaker suddenly cracked. "But that's not the *right* way to make knives," she complained shrilly. "They wouldn't balance right. I'll show you—" She snatched up two braces of knives from her workbench and let fly at a cross-shaped target across the room—not in succession, but all four arms swinging together, all four blades in the air at once. They *spunged* into the target, a blade at the extreme end of each arm of the cross. "See? You couldn't do that with a long knife. It would fight with itself and not go straight."

"Boss—" Forty-one tried again. Joe-Jim handed him a mouthful of knuckles without looking around.

"I see your point," Jim told the knifemaker, "but we don't want these knives for throwing. We want them for cutting and stabbing up close. Get on with it—I want to see the first one before you eat again."

The old woman bit her lip. "Do I get my usuals?" she said sharply.

"Certainly you get your usuals," he assured her. "A tithe on every kill till the blades are paid for—and good eating all the time you work."

She shrugged her misshapen shoulders. "O.K." She turned, tonged up a long flat fragment of steel with her two left hands and clanged the stock into the furnace. Joe-Jim turned to Forty-one.

"What is it?" Joe asked.

"Boss, Ertz sent me to get Hugh."

"Well, why didn't you do it?"

"I don't find him. Bobo says he's gone up to no-weight."

"Well, go get him. No, that won't do—you wouldn't know where to find him. I'll have to do it myself. Go back to Ertz and tell him to wait."

Forty-one hurried off. The Boss was all right, but it was not good to tarry in his presence.

"Now you've got us running errands," Jim commented sourly. "How do you like being a blood brother, Joe?"

"You got us into this."

"So? The blood-swearing was your idea."

"Damn it, you know why I did that. *They* took it seriously. And we are going to need all the help we can get, if we are to get out of this with a skin that will hold water."

"Oh? So *you* didn't take it seriously?"

"Did you?"

Jim smiled cynically. "Just about as seriously as you do, my dear, deceitful brother. As matters stand now, it is much, much healthier for you and me to keep to the bargain right up to the hilt. 'All for one and one for all.' "

"You've been reading Dumas again."

"And why not?"

"That's O.K. But don't be a damn fool about it."

"I won't be. I know which side of the blade is edged."

Joe-Jim found Squatty and Pig sleeping outside the door which led to the Control Room. He knew then that Hugh must be inside, for he had assigned the two as personal bodyguards to Hugh. It was a foregone conclusion anyhow; if Hugh had gone up to no-weight, he would be heading either for Main Drive, or the Control Room—more probably the Control Room. The place held a tremendous fascination for Hugh. Ever since the earlier time when Joe-Jim had almost literally dragged him into the Control Room and had forced him to see with his own eyes that the Ship was not the whole world but simply a vessel adrift in a much larger world—a vessel that could be driven and *moved*—ever since that time and throughout the period that followed while he was still a captured slave of Joe-Jim's, he had been obsessed with the idea of moving the Ship, of sitting at the controls and making it *go!*

It meant more to him than it could possibly have meant to a space pilot from Earth. From the time that the first rocket made the little jump from Terra to the Moon, the spaceship pilot has been the standard romantic hero whom every boy wished to emulate. But Hugh's ambition was of no such picayune caliber—he wished to move his *world*. In Earth standards and concepts it would be less ambitious to dream of equipping the Sun with jets and go gunning it around the Galaxy.

Young Archimedes had his lever; he sought a fulcrum.

Joe-Jim paused at the door of the great silver stellarium globe which constituted the Control Room and peered in. He could not see Hugh, but he knew that he must be at the controls in the chair of the chief astrogator, for the lights were being manipulated. The images of the stars were scattered over the inner surface of the sphere pro-

ducing a simulacrum of the heavens outside the Ship.
The illusion was not fully convincing from the door where
Joe-Jim rested; from the center of the sphere it would
be complete.

Sector by sector the stars snuffed out, as Hugh manipulated the controls from the center of the sphere. A
sector was left shining on the far side forward. It
was marked by a large and brilliant orb, many times as
bright as its companions. Joe-Jim ceased watching and
pulled himself hand over hand up to the control chairs.
"Hugh!" Jim called out.

"Who's there?" demanded Hugh and leaned his head
out of the deep chair. "Oh, it's you. Hello."

"Ertz wants to see you. Come on out of there."

"O.K. But come here first. I want to show you something."

"Nuts to him," Joe said to his brother. But Jim
answered, "Oh, come on and see what it is. Won't take
long."

The twins climbed into the control station and settled
down in the chair next to Hugh's. "What's up?"

"That star out there," said Hugh, pointing at the brilliant one. "It's grown bigger since the last time I was here."

"Huh? Sure it has. It's been getting brighter for a long
time. Couldn't see it at all first time I was ever in here."

"Then we're closer to it."

"Of course," agreed Joe. "I knew that. It just goes to
prove that the Ship is moving."

"But why didn't you tell me about this?"

"About what?"

"About that star. About the way it's been growing bigger."

"What difference does it make?"

"What difference does it make! Why, good Jordan, man
—that's it. That's where we're going. That's *the End of
the Trip!*"

Joe-Jim—both of him—was momentarily startled. Not
being himself concerned with any objective other than his
own safety and comfort, it was hard for him to realize that
Hugh, and perhaps Bill Ertz as well, held as their first
objective the recapturing of the lost accomplishments of

their ancestors in order to complete the long-forgotten, half-mythical Trip to Far Centaurus.

Jim recovered himself. "Hm-m-m——maybe. What makes you think that star is Far Centaurus?"

"Maybe it isn't. I don't care. But it's the star we are closest to and we are moving toward it. When we don't know which star is which, one is as good as another. Joe-Jim, the ancients must have had *some* way of telling the stars apart."

"Sure they did," Joe confirmed, "but what of it? You've picked the one you want to go to. Come on. I want to get back down."

"All right," Hugh agreed reluctantly. They began the long trip down.

Ertz sketched out to Joe-Jim and Hugh his interview with Narby. "Now my idea in coming up," he continued, "is this: I'll send Alan back down to heavy-weight with a message to Narby, telling him that I've been able to get in contact with you, Hugh, and urging him to meet us somewhere above Crew country to hear what I've found out."

"Why don't you simply go back and fetch him yourself?" objected Hugh.

Ertz looked slightly sheepish. "Because *you* tried that method on *me*—and it didn't work. You returned from mutie country and told me the wonders you had seen. I didn't believe you and had you tried for heresy. If Joe-Jim hadn't rescued you, you would have gone to the Converter. If you had not hauled me up to no-weight and forced me to see with my own eyes, I never would have believed you. I assure you Narby won't be any easier a lock to force than I was. I want to get him up here, then show him the stars and make him see—peacefully if we can; by force if we must."

"I don't get it," said Jim. "Why wouldn't it be simpler to cut his throat?"

"It would be a pleasure. But it wouldn't be smart. Narby can be a tremendous amount of help to us. Jim, if you knew the Ship's organization the way I do, you would see why. Narby carries more weight in the Council than any other Ship's officer *and* he speaks for the Captain. If we win him over, we may never have to fight at all. If we don't—well, I'm not sure of the outcome, not if we have to fight."

"I don't think he'll come up. He'll suspect a trap."

"Which is another reason why Alan must go rather than myself. He would ask me a lot of embarrassing questions and be dubious about the answers. Alan he won't expect so much of." Ertz turned to Alan and continued, "Alan you don't know anything when he asks you but just what I'm about to tell you. Savvy?"

"Sure. I don't know nothing, I ain't seen nothing, I ain't heard nothing." With frank simplicity he added, "I never did know much."

"Good. You've never laid eyes on Joe-Jim, you've never heard of the stars. You're just my messenger, a knife I took along to help me. Now here's what you are to tell him—" He gave Alan the message for Narby, couched in simple but provocative terms, then made sure that Alan had it all straight. "All right—on your way! Good eating."

Alan slapped the grip of his knife, answered, "Good eating!" and sped away.

It is not possible for a peasant to burst precipitously into the presence of the Captain's Executive—Alan found that out. He was halted by the master-at-arms on watch outside Narby's suite, cuffed around a bit for his insistence on entering, referred to a boredly unsympathetic clerk who took his name and told him to return to his village and wait to be summoned. He held his ground and insisted that he had a message of immediate importance from the Chief Engineer to Commander Narby. The clerk looked up again. "Give me the writing."

"There is no writing."

"What? That's ridiculous. There is always a writing. Regulations."

"He had no time to make a writing. He gave me a word message."

"What is it?"

Alan shook his head. "It is private, for Commander Narby only. I have orders."

The clerk looked his exasperation.

But, being only a probationer, he forewent the satisfaction of direct and immediate disciplining of the recalcitrant churl in favor of the safer course of passing the buck higher up.

The chief clerk was brief. "Give me the message."

Alan braced himself and spoke to a scientist in a fashion he had never used in his life, even to one as junior as this passed clerk. "Sir, all I ask is for you to tell Commander Narby that I have a message for him from Chief Engineer Ertz. If the message is not delivered, I won't be the one to go to the Convérter! But I don't dare give the message to anyone else."

The under official pulled at his lip, and decided to take a chance on disturbing his superior.

Alan delivered his message to Narby in a low voice in order that the orderly standing just outside the door might not overhear. Narby stared at him. "Ertz wants *me* to come along with *you* up to mutie country?"

"Not all the way up to mutie country, sir. To a point in between, where Hugh Hoyland can meet you."

Narby exhaled noisily. "It's preposterous. I'll send a squad of knives up to fetch him down to me."

Alan delivered the balance of his message. This time he carefully raised his voice to ensure that the orderly, and, if possible, others might hear his words. "Ertz said to tell you that if you were *afraid* to go, just to forget the whole matter. He will take it up with the Council himself."

Alan owed his continued existence thereafter to the fact that Narby was the sort of man who lived by shrewdness rather than by direct force. Narby's knife was at his belt; Alan was painfully aware that he had been required to deposit his own with the master-at-arms.

Narby controlled his expression. He was too intelligent to attribute the insult to the oaf before him, though he promised himself to give said oaf a little special attention at a more convenient time. Pique, curiosity, and potential loss of face all entered into his decision. "I'm coming with you," he said savagely. "I want to ask him if you got his message straight."

Narby considered having a major guard called out to accompany him, but he discarded the idea. Not only would it make the affair extremely public before he had an opportunity to judge its political aspects, but also it would lose him almost as much face as simply refusing to go. But he inquired nervously of Alan as Alan retrieved his weapon from the master-at-arms, "You're a good knife?"

"None better," Alan agreed cheerfully.

Narby hoped that the man was not simply boastful. Muties—Narby wished that he himself had found more time lately for practice in the manly arts.

Narby gradually regained his composure as he followed Alan up toward low-weight. In the first place nothing happened, no alarms; in the second place Alan was obviously a cautious and competent scout, one who moved alertly and noiselessly and never entered a deck without pausing to peer cautiously around before letting his body follow his eye. Narby might have been more nervous had he heard what Alan did hear—little noises from the depths of the great dim passageways, rustlings which told him that their progress was flanked on all sides. This worried Alan subconsciously, although he had expected something of the sort—he knew that both Hugh and Joe-Jim were careful captains who would not neglect to cover an approach. He would have worried more if he had *not* been able to detect a reconnaissance which should have been present.

When he approached the rendezvous some twenty decks above the highest civilized level, he stopped and whistled. A whistle answered him. "It's Alan," he called out.

"Come up and show yourself." Alan did so, without neglecting his usual caution. When he saw no one but his friends—Ertz, Hugh, Joe-Jim, and Bobo, he motioned for Narby to follow him.

The sight of Joe-Jim and Bobo broke Narby's restored calm with a sudden feeling that he had been trapped. He snatched at his knife and backed clumsily down the stairs —turned. Bobo's knife was out even faster. For a split moment the outcome hung balanced, ready to fall either way. But Joe-Jim slapped Bobo across the face, took his knife from him and let it clatter to the deck, then relieved him of his slingshot.

Narby was in full flight, with Hugh and Ertz calling vainly after him. "Fetch him, Bobo!" Jim commanded, "and don't hurt him." Bobo lumbered away.

He was back in fairly short order. "Run fast," he commented. He dropped Narby to the deck where the officer lay almost quiet while he fought to catch his breath. Bobo took Narby's knife from his own belt and tried it by shaving coarse black hairs from his left forearm. "Good blade," he approved.

"Give it back to him," Jim ordered. Bobo looked extremely startled but complied wistfully. Joe-Jim returned Bobo's own weapons to him.

Narby matched Bobo's surprise at regaining his sidearm, but he concealed it better. He even managed to accept it with dignity.

"Look," Ertz began in worried tones, "I'm sorry you got your wind up, Fin. Bobo's not a bad sort. It was the only way to get you back."

Narby fought with himself to regain the cool self-discipline with which he habitually met the world. Damn! he told himself, this situation is preposterous. Well—"Forget it," he said shortly. "I was expecting to meet you; I didn't expect a bunch of armed muties. You have an odd taste in playmates, Ertz."

"Sorry," Bill Ertz replied, "I guess I should have warned you"—a piece of mendacious diplomacy. "But they're all right. Bobo you've met. This is Joe-Jim. He's a . . . a sort of a Ship's officer among the muties."

"Good eating," Joe acknowledged politely.

"Good eating," Narby replied mechanically.

"Hugh you know, I think." Narby agreed that he did. An embarrassed pause followed. Narby broke it.

"Well," he said, "you must have had some reason to send word for me to come up here. Or was it just to play games?"

"I did," Ertz agreed. "I —Shucks, I hardly know where to start. See here, Narby, you won't believe this, but I've *seen*. Everything Hugh told us was true. I've been in the Control Room. I've seen the stars. I *know*."

Narby stared at him. "Ertz," he said slowly, "you've gone out of your mind."

Hugh Hoyland spoke up excitedly. "That's because you haven't *seen*. It *moves*, I tell you. The Ship *moves* like a—"

"I'll handle this," Ertz cut in. "Listen to me, Narby. What it all means you will soon decide for yourself, but

I can tell you what I saw. They took me up to no-weight and into the Captain's veranda. That's a compartment with a glass wall. You can stare right out through into a great black empty space—big—bigger than anything could be. Bigger than the Ship. And there were lights out there, stars, just like the ancient myths said."

Narby looked both amazed and disgusted. "Where's your logic, man? I thought you were a scientist. What do you mean, 'bigger than the Ship'? That's an absurdity, a contradiction in terms. By definition, the Ship is the Ship. All else is a part of it."

Ertz shrugged helplessly. "I know it sounds that way. I can't explain it; it defies all logic. It's— Oh, Huff! You'll know what I mean when you see it."

"Control yourself," Narby advised him. "Don't talk nonsense. A thing is logical or it isn't. For a thing to be it must occupy space. You've seen, or thought you saw, something remarkable, but whatever it was, it can be no larger than the compartment it was in. You can't show me anything that contradicts an obvious fact of nature."

"I told you I couldn't explain it."

"Of course you can't."

The twins had been whispering disgustedly, one head to the other. "Stop the chatter," Joe said in louder tones. "We're ready to go. Come on."

"Sure," Ertz agreed eagerly, "let's drop it, Narby, until you have seen it. Come on now—it's a long climb."

"What?" Narby demanded. "Say, what is this? Go where?"

"Up to the Captain's veranda, and the Control Room."

"Me? Don't be ridiculous. I'm going down at once."

"No, Narby," Ertz denied. "That's why I sent for you. You've got to see."

"Don't be silly—I don't need to see; common sense gives sufficient answer. However," he went on, "I do want to congratulate you on making a friendly contact with the muties. We should be able to work out some means of cooperation. I think—"

Joe-Jim took one step forward. "You're wasting time," he said evenly. "We're going up—you, too. I really do insist."

Narby shook his head. "It's out of the question. Some

other time, perhaps, after we have worked out a method of cooperation."

Hugh stepped in closer to him from the other side. "You don't seem to understand. You're going *now*."

Narby glanced the other way at Ertz. Ertz nodded. "That's how it is, Narby."

Narby cursed himself silently. Great Jordan! What in the Ship was he thinking of to let himself get into such a position? He had a distinct feeling that the two-headed man would rather that he showed fight. Impossible, preposterous situation. He cursed again to himself, but gave way as gracefully as he could. "Oh, well! Rather than cause an argument I'll go now. Let's get on with it. Which way?"

"Just stick with me," advised Ertz. Joe-Jim whistled loudly in a set pattern. Muties seemed to grow out of the floor plates, the bulkheads, the overhead, until six or eight more had been added to the party. Narby was suddenly sick with the full realization of just how far he had strayed from the way of caution. The party moved up.

It took them a long time to get up to no-weight, as Narby was not used to climbing. The steady reduction in weight as they rose from deck to deck relieved him somewhat but the help afforded was more than offset by the stomach qualms he felt as weight dropped away from him. He did not have a true attack of space-sickness—like all born in the Ship, muties and Crew, he was more or less acclimated to lessened weight, but he had done practically no climbing since reckless adolescence. By the time they reached the innermost deck of the Ship he was acutely uncomfortable and hardly able to proceed.

Joe-Jim sent the added members of the party back below and told Bobo to carry Narby. Narby waved him away. "I can make it," he protested, and by sheer stubborn will forced his body to behave. Joe-Jim looked him over and countermanded the order. By the time a long series of gliding dives had carried them as far forward as the transverse bulkhead beyond which lay the Control Room, he was reasonably comfortable again.

They did not stop first at the Control Room, but, in accordance with a plan of Hugh's, continued on to the Captain's veranda. Narby was braced for what he saw there, not only by Ertz's confused explanation, but because

Hugh had chattered buoyantly to him about it all the latter part of the trip. Hugh was feeling warmly friendly to Narby by the time they arrived—it was wonderful to have somebody to listen!

Hugh floated in through the door ahead of the others, executed a neat turn in mid-air, and steadied himself with one hand on the back of the Captain's easy chair. With the other he waved at the great view port and the starry firmament beyond it. "There it is!" he exulted. "There it is. Look at it—isn't it wonderful?"

Narby's face showed no expression, but he looked long and intently at the brilliant display. "Remarkable," he conceded at last, "remarkable. I've never seen anything like it."

" 'Remarkable' ain't half," protested Hugh. "Wonderful is the word."

"O.K.—'wonderful,' " Narby assented. "Those bright little lights—you say those are the stars that the ancients talked about?"

"Why, yes," agreed Hugh, feeling slightly disconcerted without knowing why, "only they're not little. They are big, enormous things, like the Ship. They just look little because they are so far away. See that very bright one, that big one, down to the left? It looks big because it's closer. I *think* that is Far Centaurus—but I'm not sure," he admitted in a burst of frankness.

Narby glanced quickly at him, then back to the big star. "How far away is it?"

"I don't know. But I'll find out. There are instruments to measure such things in the Control Room, but I haven't got the hang of them entirely. It doesn't matter, though. We'll get there yet!"

"Huh?"

"Sure. Finish the Trip."

Narby looked blank, but said nothing. His was a careful and orderly mind, logical to a high degree. He was a capable executive and could make rapid decisions when necessary, but he was by nature inclined to reserve his opinions when possible, until he had had time to chew over the data and assess it.

He was even more taciturn in the Control Room. He listened and looked, but asked very few questions. Hugh did not care. This was his toy, his gadget, his baby. To show it off to someone who had never seen it and who would listen was all he asked.

At Ertz's suggestion the party stopped at Joe-Jim's apartment on the way back down. Narby must be committed to the same course of action as the blood brotherhood and plans must be made to carry out such action, if the stratagem which brought Narby to them was to be fruitful. Narby agreed to stop unreluctantly, having become convinced of the reality of the truce under which he made this unprecedented sortie into mutie country. He listened quietly while Ertz outlined what they had in mind. He was still quiet when Ertz had finished.

"Well?" said Ertz at last, when the silence had dragged on long enough to get on his nerves.

"You expect some comment from me?"

"Yes, of course. You figure into it." Narby knew that he did and knew that an answer was expected from him; he was stalling for time.

"Well—" Narby pursed his lips and fitted his fingertips together. "It seems to me that this problem divides itself into two parts. Hugh Hoyland, as I understand it, your purpose of carrying out the ancient Plan of Jordan cannot be realized until the Ship as a whole is pacified and brought under one rule—you need order and discipline for your purpose from Crew country clear to the Control Room. Is that right?"

"Certainly. We have to man the Main Drive and that means—"

"Please. Frankly, I am not qualified to understand things that I have seen so recently and have had no opportunity to study. As to your chances of success in that project, I would prefer to rely on the opinion of the Chief Engineer. Your problem is the second phase; it appears that you are necessarily interested in the first phase."

"Of course."

"Then let's talk about the first phase only. It involves matters of public policy and administration—I feel more at home there; perhaps my advice will be useful. Joe-Jim, I understand that you are looking for an opportunity to effect a peace between the muties and the members of the Crew—peace and good eating? Right?"

"That's correct," Jim agreed.

"Good. It has been my purpose for a long time and that of many of the Ship's officers. Frankly it never occurred to me that it could be achieved other than by sheer force. We had steeled ourselves to the prospect of a long and difficult and bloody war. The records of the oldest Witness, handed down to him by his predecessors clear back to the time of the mythical Mutiny, make no mention of anything but war between muties and the Crew. But this is a better way—I am delighted."

"Then you're with us!" exclaimed Ertz.

"Steady—there are many other things to be considered. Ertz, you and I know, and Hoyland as well I should think, that not all of the Ship's officers will agree with us. What of that?"

"That's easy," put in Hugh Hoyland. "Bring them up to no-weight one at a time, let them see the stars and learn the truth."

Narby shook his head. "You have the litter carrying the porters. I told you this problem is in two phases. There is no point in trying to convince a man of something he won't believe when you need him to agree to something he can understand. *After* the Ship is consolidated it will be simple enough then to let the officers experience the Control Room and the stars."

"But—"

"He's right," Ertz stopped him. "No use getting cluttered up with a lot of religious issues when the immediate problem is a practical one. There are numerous officers whom we could get on our side for the purpose of pacifying the Ship who would raise all kinds of fuss if we tackled them first on the idea that the Ship *moves*."

"But—"

"No 'buts' about it. Narby is right. It's common sense. Now, Narby—about this matter of those officers who may not be convinced—here's how we see it: In the first place it's your business and mine to win over as many as we can. Any who hold out against us—well, the Converter is always hungry."

Narby nodded, completely undismayed by the idea of assassination as a policy. "That seems the safest plan. Mightn't it be a little bit difficult?"

"That is where Joe-Jim comes in. We'll have the best knives in the Ship to back us up."

"I see. Joe-Jim is, I take it, Boss of all the muties?"

"What gave you that idea?" growled Joe, vexed without knowing why.

"Why, I supposed . . . I was given to understand—" Narby stopped. No one had *told* him that Joe-Jim was king of the upper decks; he had assumed it from appearances. He felt suddenly very uneasy. Had he been negotiating uselessly? What was the point in a pact with this two-headed monstrosity if he did not speak for the muties?

"I should have made that clear," Ertz said hastily. "Joe-Jim helps us to establish a new administration, then we will be able to back him up with knives to pacify the rest of the muties. Joe-Jim isn't Boss of all the muties, but he has the largest, strongest gang. With our help he soon will be Boss of all of them."

Narby quickly adjusted his mind to the new data. Muties against muties, with only a little help from the cadets of the Crew, seemed to him a good way to fight. On second thoughts, it was better than an outright truce at once—for there would be fewer muties to administer when it was all over, less chance of another mutiny. "I see," he agreed. "So— Have you considered what the situation will be afterwards?"

"What do you mean?" inquired Hoyland.

"Can you picture the present Captain carrying out these plans?"

Ertz saw what he was driving at, and so did Hoyland—vaguely.

"Go on," said Ertz.

"*Who is to be the new Captain?*" Narby looked squarely at Ertz.

Ertz had not thought the matter through; he realized now that the question was very pertinent, if the *coup d'état* was not to be followed by a bloody scramble for power. He had permitted himself to dream of being selected as Captain—sometime. But he knew that Narby was pointed that way, too.

Ertz had been as honestly struck by the romantic notion of moving the Ship as Hoyland. He realized that his old ambition stood in the way of the new; he renounced the old with only a touch of wistfulness.

"You will have to be Captain, Fin. Are you willing to be?"

Phineas Narby accepted gracefully. "I suppose so, if that's the way you want it. You would make a fine Captain yourself, Ertz."

Ertz shook his head, understanding perfectly that Narby's full cooperation turned on this point. "I'll continue as Chief Engineer—I want to handle the Main Drive for the Trip."

"Slow down!" Joe interrupted. "I don't agree to this. Why should *he* be Captain?"

Narby faced him. "Do you want to be Captain?" He kept his voice carefully free of sarcasm. A mutie for Captain!

"Huff's name—no! But why should you be? Why not Ertz or Hugh?"

"Not me," Hugh disclaimed. "I'll have no time for administration. I'm the astrogator."

"Seriously, Joe-Jim," Ertz explained, "Narby is the only one of the group who can get the necessary cooperation out of the Ship's officers."

"Damn it—if they won't cooperate we can slit their throats."

"With Narby as Captain we won't have to slit throats."

"I don't like it," groused Joe. His brother shushed him. "Why get excited about it, Joe? Jordan knows *we* don't want the responsibility."

"I quite understand your misgivings," Narby suggested suavely, "but I don't think you need worry. I would be forced to depend on you, of course, to administer the muties. I would administer the lower decks, a job I am used to, and you would be Vice-Captain, if you are willing to serve, for the muties. It would be folly for me to attempt to administer directly a part of the Ship I'm not familiar with and people whose customs I don't know. I really can't accept the captaincy unless you are willing to help me in that fashion. Will you do it?"

"I don't want any part of it," protested Joe.

"I'm sorry. Then I must refuse to be Captain—I really can't undertake it if you won't help me that much."

"Oh, go ahead, Joe," Jim insisted. "Let's take it—for the time being at least. The job has to be done."

"All right," Joe capitulated, "but I don't like it."

Narby ignored the fact that Joe-Jim had not specifically agreed to Narby's elevation to the captaincy; no further mention was made of it.

The discussion of ways and means was tedious and need not be repeated. It was agreed that Ertz, Alan, and Narby should all return to their usual haunts and occupations while preparations were made to strike.

Hugh detailed a guard to see them safely down to high-weight. "You'll send Alan up when you are ready?" he said to Narby as they were about to leave.

"Yes," Narby agreed, "but don't expect him soon. Ertz and I will have to have time to feel out friends—and there's the matter of the old Captain, I'll have to persuade him to call a meeting of all the Ship's officers—he's never too easy to handle."

"Well, that's your job. Good eating!"

"Good eating."

On the few occasions when the scientist priests who ruled the Ship under Jordan's Captain met in full assembly they gathered in a great hall directly above the Ship's offices on the last civilized deck. Forgotten generations past, before the time of the mutiny led by Ship's Metalsmith Roy Huff, the hall had been a gymnasium, a place for fun and healthy exercise, as planned by the designers of the great starship—but the present users knew nothing of that.

Narby watched the roster clerk check off the Ship's officers as they arrived, worried under a bland countenance. There were only a few more to arrive; he would soon have no excuse not to notify the Captain that the meeting was ready—but he had received no word from Joe-Jim and Hoyland. Had that fool Alan managed to get himself killed on the way up to deliver the word? Had he fallen and broken his worthless neck? Was he dead with a mutie's knife in his belly?

Ertz came in, and before seeking his seat among the department heads, went up to where Narby sat in front of the Captain's chair. "How about it?" he inquired softly.

"All right," Narby told him, "but no word yet."

"Hm-m-m——" Ertz turned around and assayed his support in the crowd. Narby did likewise. Not a majority, not a *certain* majority, for anything as drastic as this. Still——the issue would not depend on voting.

The roster clerk touched his arm. "All present, sir, except those excused for sickness, and one on watch at the Converter."

Narby directed that the Captain be notified, with a sick feeling that something had gone wrong. The Captain, as usual, with complete disregard for the comfort and convenience of others, took his time about appearing. Narby was glad of the delay, but miserable in enduring it. When the old man finally waddled in, flanked by his orderlies, and settled heavily into his chair, he was, again as usual, impatient to get the meeting over. He waved for the others to be seated and started in on Narby.

"Very well, Commander Narby, let's have the agenda—you have an agenda, I hope?"

"Yes, Captain, there is an agenda."

"Then have it read, man, have it read! Why are you delaying?"

"Yes, sir." Narby turned to the reading clerk and handed him a sheaf of writings. The clerk glanced at them, looked puzzled, but, receiving no encouragement from Narby, commenced to read: "Petition, to Council and Captain: Lieutenant Braune, administrator of the village of Sector 9, being of frail health and advanced age, prays that he be relieved of all duty and retired——" The clerk continued, setting forth the recommendations of the officers and departments concerned.

The Captain twisted impatiently in his chair, finally interrupted the reading. "What's is this, Narby? Can't you handle routine matters without all this fuss?"

"I understood that the Captain was displeased with the fashion in which a similar matter was lately handled. I have no wish to trespass on the Captain's prerogatives."

"Nonsense, man! Don't read Regulations to me. Let the Council act, then bring their decision to me for review."

"Yes, sir." Narby took the writing from the clerk and gave him another. The clerk read.

It was an equally fiddling matter. Sector 3 village, because of an unexplained blight which had infected their hydroponic farms, prayed for relief and a suspension of taxes. The Captain put up with still less of this item before interrupting. Narby would have been sorely pressed for any excuse to continue the meeting had not the word he awaited arrived at that moment. It was a mere scrap of parchment, brought in from outside the hall by one of his own men. It contained the single word, "Ready." Narby looked at it, nodded to Ertz, and addressed the Captain:

"Sir, since you have no wish to listen to the petitions of your Crew, I will continue at once with the main business of this meeting." The veiled insolence of the statement caused the Captain to stare at him suspiciously, but Narby went on. "For many generations, through the lives of a succession of Witnesses, the Crew has suffered from the depredations of the muties. Our livestock, our children, even our own persons, have been in constant jeopardy. Jordan's Regulations are not honored above the levels where we live. Jordan's Captain himself is not free to travel in the upper levels of the Ship.

"It has been an article of faith that Jordan so ordained it, that the children pay with blood for the sins of their ancestors. It was the will of Jordan—we were told.

"I, for one, have never been reconciled to this constant drain on the Ship's mass." He paused.

The old Captain had been having some difficulty in believing his ears. But he found his voice. Pointing, he squealed, "Do you dispute the Teachings?"

"I do not. I maintain that the Teachings do not command us to leave the muties outside the Regulations, and never did. I demand that they be brought under the Regulations!"

"You . . . you— You are relieved of duty, sir!"

"Not," answered Narby, his insolence now overt, "until I have had my say."

"Arrest that man!" But the Captain's orderlies stood fast, though they shuffled and looked unhappy—Narby himself had selected them.

Narby turned back to the amazed Council, and caught the eye of Ertz. "All right," he said. "Now!" Ertz got up and trotted toward the door. Narby continued, "Many of you think as I do, but we always supposed that we would have to fight for it. With the help of Jordan, I have been able to establish a contact with the muties and arrange a

truce. Their leaders are coming here to negotiate with us.
There!" He pointed dramatically at the door.

Ertz reappeared; following him came Hugh Hoyland,
Joe-Jim, and Bobo. Hoyland turned to the right along
the wall and circled the company. He was followed single
file by a string of muties—Joe-Jim's best butcher boys.
Another such column trailed after Joe-Jim and Bobo to
the left.

Joe-Jim, Hugh, and half a dozen more in each wing
were covered with crude armor which extended below their
waists. The armor was topped off with clumsy helms, lat-
ticeworks of steel, which protected their heads without
greatly interfering with vision. Each of the armored ones,
a few of the others, carried unheard-of knives—long as
a man's arm!

The startled officers might have stopped the invasion
at the bottleneck through which it entered had they been
warned and led. But they were disorganized, helpless, and
their strongest leaders had invited the invaders in. They
shifted in their chairs, reached for their knives, and glanced
anxiously from one to another. But no one made the first
move which would start a general bloodletting.

Narby turned to the Captain. "What about it? Do you
receive this delegation in peace?"

It seemed likely that age and fat living would keep the
Captain from answering, from ever answering anything
again. But he managed to croak, "Get 'em out of here!
Get 'em out! You— You'll make the Trip for this!"

Narby turned back to Joe-Jim and jerked his thumb upward. Jim spoke to Bobo—and a knife was buried to
the grip in the Captain's fat belly. He squawked, rather
than screamed, and a look of utter bewilderment spread
over his features. He plucked awkwardly at the hilt as
if to assure himself that it was really there. "Mutiny—"
he stated. "Mutiny—" The word trailed off as he collapsed
into his chair, and fell heavily forward to the deck on his
face.

Narby shoved it with his foot and spoke to the two orderlies. "Carry it outside," he commanded. They obeyed,
seeming relieved at having something to do and someone

to tell them to do it. Narby turned back to the silent watching mass. "Does anyone else object to a peace with the
muties?"

An elderly officer, one who had dreamed away his life
as judge and spiritual adviser to a remote village, stood
up and pointed a bony finger at Narby, while his white
beard jutted indignantly. "Jordan will punish you for this!
Mutiny and sin—the spirit of Huff!"

Narby nodded to Joe-Jim; the old man's words gurgled
in his throat, the point of a blade sticking out under one
ear. Bobo looked pleased with himself.

"There has been enough talk," Narby announced. "It
is better to have a little blood now than much blood later.
Let those who stand with me in this matter get up and come
forward."

Ertz set the precedent by striding forward and urging
his surest personal supporters to come with him. Reaching
the front of the room, he pulled out his knife and raised
the point. "I salute Phineas Narby, Jordan's Captain!"

His own supporters were left with no choice. "Phineas
Narby, Jordan's Captain!"

The hard young men in Narby's clique—the backbone
of the dissident rationalist bloc among the scientist priests
—joined the swing forward *en masse,* points raised high
and shouting for the new Captain. The undecided and the
opportunists hastened to join, as they saw which side of
the blade was edged. When the division was complete,
there remained a handful only of Ship's officers still hang-
ing back, almost all of whom were either elderly or hyper-
religious.

Ertz watched Captain Narby look them over, then pick
up Joe-Jim with his eyes. Ertz put a hand on his arm.
"There are few of them and practically helpless," he pointed
out. "Why not disarm them and let them retire?"

Narby gave him an unfriendly look. "Let them stay alive
and breed mutiny. I am quite capable of making my own
decisions, Ertz."

Ertz bit his lip. "Very well, Captain."

"That's better." He signaled to Joe-Jim.

The long knives made short work.

Hugh hung back from the slaughter. His old teacher,

Lieutenant Nelson, the village scientist who had seen his ability and selected him for scientisthood, was one of the group. It was a factor he had not anticipated.

World conquest—and consolidation. Faith, or the Sword. Joe-Jim's bullies, amplified by hot-blooded young cadets supplied by Captain Narby, combed the middle decks and the upper decks. The muties, individualists by the very nature of their existence and owing no allegiance higher than that to the leaders of their gangs, were no match for the planned generalship of Joe-Jim, nor did their weapons match the strange, long knives that bit before a man was ready.

The rumor spread through mutie country that it was better to surrender quietly to the gang of the Two Wise-Heads—good eating for those who surrendered, death inescapable for those who did not.

But it was nevertheless a long slow process—there were so many, many decks, so many miles of gloomy corridors, so many countless compartments in which unreconstructed muties might lurk. Furthermore, the process grew slower as it advanced, as Joe-Jim attempted to establish a police patrol, an interior guard, over each sector, deck, and stairway trunk, as fast as his striking groups mopped them up.

To Narby's disappointment, the two-headed man was not killed in his campaigns. Joe-Jim had learned from his own books that a general need not necessarily expose himself to direct combat.

Hugh buried himself in the Control Room. Not only was he more interested in the subtle problems of mastering the how and why of the complex controls and the parallel complexity of starship ballistics, but also the whole matter of the blood purge was distasteful to him—because of Lieutenant Nelson. Violence and death he was used to; they were commonplace even on the lower levels—but the incident made him vaguely unhappy, even though his own evaluations were not sufficiently clean-cut for him to feel personal responsibility for the old man's death.

He just wished it had not happened.

But the controls—ah! There was something a man could put his heart into. He was attempting a task that an Earthman would have rejected as impossible—an Earthman would have *known* that the piloting and operation of an interstellar ship was a task so difficult that the best possible technical education combined with extensive experience in the handling of lesser spacecraft would constitute a barely adequate grounding for additional intensive highly specialized training for the task.

Hugh Hoyland did not know that. So he went ahead and did it anyhow.

In which attempt he was aided by the genius of the designers. The *controls* of most machinery may be considered under the head of simple pairs, stop-and-go, push-and-pull, up-and-down, in-and-out, on-and-off, right-and-left, their permutations and combinations. The real difficulties have to do with upkeep and repair, adjustment and replacements.

But the controls and main drive machinery of the starship *Vanguard* required no upkeep and no repair; their complexities were below the molar level, they contained no moving parts, friction took no toll and they did not fall out of adjustment. Had it been necessary for him to understand and repair the machines he dealt with, it would have been impossible. A fourteen-year-old child may safely be entrusted with a family skycar and be allowed to make thousand-mile jaunts overnight unaccompanied; it is much more probable that he will injure himself on the trip by overeating than by finding some way to mismanage or damage the vehicle. But if the skycar *should* fall out of adjustment, ground itself, and signal for a repair crew, the repair crew is essential; the child cannot fix it himself.

The *Vanguard* needed no repair crew—save for nonessential auxiliary machinery such as transbelts, elevators, automassagers, dining services, and the like. Such machinery which necessarily used moving parts had worn out before the time of the first Witness; the useless mass involved had gone into the auxiliary Converter, or had been adapted to other simpler purposes. Hugh was not even aware that there ever had been such machinery; the stripped condition of most compartments was a simple fact of nature to him, no cause for wonder.

Hugh was aided in his quest for understanding by two other facts:

First, spaceship ballistics is a very simple subject, being

hardly more than the application of the second law
of motion to an inverse-square field. That statement runs
contrary to our usual credos; it happens to be true. Baking
a cake calls for much greater, though subconscious, knowledge of engineering; knitting a sweater requires a grasp
of much more complex mathematical relationships. The
topology of a knitted garment—but try it yourself sometime!

For a complex subject, consider neurology, or cata-
lysts—but don't mention ballistics.

Second, the designers had clearly in mind that the *Vanguard* would reach her destination not sooner than two
generations after her departure; they wished to make things
easy for the then-not-yet-born pilots who would control
her on arrival. Although they anticipated no such hiatus
in technical culture as took place, they did their best to
make the controls simple, self-explanatory, and foolproof.
The sophisticated fourteen-year-old mentioned above
oriented as he would be to the concept of space travel,
would doubtless have figured them out in a few hours.
Hugh, reared in a culture which believed that the Ship was
the whole world, made no such quick job of it.

He was hampered by two foreign concepts, *deep* space
and *metrical* time. He had to learn to operate the distance
finder, a delayed-action, long-base, parallax type especially
designed for the *Vanguard,* and had taken readings
on a couple of dozen stellar bodies before it occurred to
him that the results he was getting could possibly mean
anything. The readings were in parsecs and meaningless
emotionally. The attempt with the aid of the Sacred books
to translate his readings into linear units he could understand resulted in figures which he felt sure were wrong,
obviously preposterous. Check and recheck, followed by
long periods of brooding, forced him unwillingly into some
dim comprehension of astronomical magnitudes.

The concepts frightened him and bewildered him. For
a period of several sleeps he stayed away from the Control
Room, and gave way to a feeling of futility and defeat.
He occupied the time in sorting over the women available;
it being the first time since his capture by Joe-Jim long ago
that he had had both the opportunity and the mood to

consider the subject. The candidates were numerous, for, in addition to the usual crop of village maidens, Joe-Jim's military operations had produced a number of prime widows. Hugh availed himself of his leading position in the Ship's new setup to select two women. The first was a widow, a strong competent woman, adept at providing a man with domestic comforts. He set her up in his new apartment, high up in low-weight, gave her a free hand, and allowed her to retain her former name of Chloe.

The other was a maiden, untrained and wild as a mutie. Hugh could not have told himself why he picked her. Certainly she had no virtues, but—she made him feel funny. She had bitten him while he was inspecting her; he had slapped her, naturally, and that should have been an end to the matter. But he sent word back later for her father to send her along.

He had not got around to naming her.

Metrical time caused him as much mental confusion as astronomical distances, but no emotional upset. The trouble was again the lack of the concept in the Ship. The Crew had the notion of topological time; they understood "now," "before," "after," "has been," "will be," even such notions as long time and short time, but the notion of measured time had dropped out of the culture. The lowest of earthbound cultures has some idea of measured time, even if limited to days and seasons, but every earthly concept of measured time originates in astronomical phenomena—the Crew had been insulated from all astronomical phenomena for uncounted generations.

Hugh had before him, on the control consoles, the only working timepieces in the Ship—but it was a long, long time before he grasped what they were for, and what bearing they had on other instruments. But until he did, he could not control the Ship. Speed, and its derivatives, acceleration and flexure, are based on *measured* time.

But when these two new concepts were finally grasped, chewed over, and ancient books reread in the light of these concepts, he was, in a greatly restricted and theoretical sense, an astrogator.

Hugh sought out Joe-Jim to ask him a question. Joe-

Jim's minds were brilliantly penetrating when he cared to exert himself; he remained a superficial dilettante because he rarely cared.

Hugh found Narby just leaving. In order to conduct the campaign of pacification of the muties it had been necessary for Narby and Joe-Jim to confer frequently; to their mutual surprise they got along well together. Narby was a capable administrator, able to delegate authority and not given to useless elbow jogging; Joe-Jim surprised and pleased Narby by being more able than any subordinate he had ever dealt with before. There was no love wasted between them, but each recognized in the other both intelligence and a hard self-interest which matched his own. There was respect and grudging contemptuous liking.

"Good eating, Captain," Hugh greeted Narby formally.

"Oh—hello, Hugh," Narby answered, then turned back to Joe-Jim. "I'll expect a report, then."

"You'll get it," Joe agreed. "There can't be more than a few dozen stragglers. We'll hunt them out, or starve them."

"Am I butting in?" Hugh asked.

"No—I'm just leaving. How goes the great work, my dear fellow?" He smiled irritatingly.

"Well enough, but slowly. Do you wish a report?"

" No hurry. Oh, by the bye, I've made the Control Room and Main Drive, in fact the entire level of no-weight, taboo for everyone, muties and Crew alike."

"So? I see your point, I guess. There is no need for any but officers to go up there."

"You don't understand me. It is a general taboo, applying to officers as well. Not to ourselves, of course."

"But . . . but —That won't work. The only effective way to convince the officers of the truth is to take them up and show them the stars!"

"That's exactly my point. I can't have my officers upset by disturbing ideas while I am consolidating my administration. It will create religious differences and impair discipline."

Hugh was too upset and astounded to answer at once. "But," he said at last, "but that's the *point*. That's why you were made Captain."

"And as Captain I will have to be the final judge of policy. The matter is closed. You are not to take anyone to the Control Room, nor any part of no-weight, until I deem it advisable. You'll have to wait."

"It's a good idea, Hugh," Jim commented. "We shouldn't stir things up while we've got a war to attend to."

"Let me get this straight," Hugh persisted. "You mean this is a temporary policy?"

"You could put it that way."

"Well—all right," Hugh conceded. "But wait—Ertz and I need to train assistants at once."

"Very well. Nominate them to me and I'll pass on them. Whom do you have in mind?"

Hugh thought. He did not actually need assistance himself; although the Control Room contained acceleration chairs for half a dozen, one man, seated in the chief astrogator's chair, could pilot the Ship. The same applied to Ertz in the Main Drive station, save in one respect. "How about Ertz? He needs porters to move mass to the Main Drive."

"Let him. I'll sign the writing. See that he uses porters from the former muties—but no one goes to the Control Room save those who have been there before." Narby turned and left with an air of dismissal.

Hugh watched him leave, then said, "I don't like this, Joe-Jim."

"Why not?" Jim asked. "It's reasonable."

"Perhaps it is. But—well, damn it! It seems to me, somehow, that truth ought to be free to anyone—any time!" He threw up his hands in a gesture of baffled exasperation.

Joe-Jim looked at him oddly. "What a curious idea," said Joe.

"Yeah, I know. It's not common sense, but it seems like it ought to be. Oh, well, forget it! That's not what I came to see you about."

"What's on your mind, Bud?"

"How do we— Look, we finish the Trip; see? We've got the Ship touching a planet, like this—" He brought his two fists together.

"Yes. Go on."

"Well, when that's done, *how do we get out of the Ship?*"

The twins looked confused, started to argue between themselves. Finally Joe interrupted his brother. "Wait a bit, Jim. Let's be logical about this. It was intended for us to get out—that implies a door, doesn't it?"

"Yeah. Sure."

"There's no door up here. It must be down in high-weight."

"But it isn't," objected Hugh. "All that country is known. There isn't any door. It has to be up in mutie country."

"In that case," Joe continued, "it should be either all the way forward, or all the way aft—otherwise it would not go anywhere. It isn't aft. There's nothing back of Main Drive but solid bulkheads. It would need to be forward."

"That's silly," Jim commented. "There's the Control Room and the Captain's veranda. That's all."

"Oh, yeah? How about the locked compartments?"

"Those aren't doors—not to the Outside anyway. That bulkhead's abaft the Control Room."

"No, stupid, but they might lead to doors."

"Stupid, eh? Even so, how are you going to open them—answer me that, bright boy?"

"What," demanded Hugh, "*are* the 'locked compartments'?"

"Don't you know? There are seven doors, spaced around the main shaft in the same bulkhead as the door to the Main Control Room. We've never been able to open them."

"Well, maybe that's what we're looking for. Let's go see!"

"It's a waste of time," Jim insisted.

But they went.

Bobo was taken along to try his monstrous strength on the doors. But even his knotted swollen muscles could not budge the levers which appeared to be intended to actuate the doors. "Well?" Jim sneered to his brother. "You see?"

Joe shrugged. "O.K.—you win. Let's go down."

"Wait a little," Hugh pleaded. "The second door back—the handle seemed to turn a little. Let's try it again."

"I'm afraid it's useless," Jim commented. But Joe said, "Oh, all right, as long as we're here."

Bobo tried again, wedging his shoulder under the lever

and pushing from his knees. The lever gave suddenly, but the door did not open. "He's broken it," Joe announced.

"Yeah," Hugh acknowledged. "I guess that's that." He placed his hand against the door.

It swung open easily.

The door did not lead to outer space, which was well for the three, for nothing in their experience warned them against the peril of the outer vacuum. Instead a very short and narrow vestibule led them to another door which was just barely ajar. The door stuck on its hinges, but the fact that it was slightly ajar prevented it from binding anywhere else. Perhaps the last man to use it left it so as a precaution against the metal surfaces freezing together—but no one would ever know.

Bobo's uncouth strength opened it easily. Another door lay six feet beyond. "I don't understand this," complained Jim, as Bobo strained at the third door. "What's the sense in an endless series of doors?"

"Wait and find out," advised his brother.

Beyond the third door lay, not another door, but a compartment, a group of compartments, odd ones, small, crowded together and of unusual shapes. Bobo shot on ahead and explored the place, knife in teeth, his ugly body almost graceful in flight. Hugh and Joe-Jim proceeded more slowly, their eyes caught by the strangeness of the place.

Bobo returned, killed his momentum skillfully against a bulkhead, took his blade from his teeth, and reported, "No door. No more door any place. Bobo look."

"There *has* to be," Hugh insisted, irritated at the dwarf for demolishing his hopes.

The moron shrugged. "Bobo look."

"We'll look." Hugh and the twins moved off in different directions, splitting the reconnaissance between them.

Hugh found no door, but what he did find interested him even more—an impossibility. He was about to shout for Joe-Jim, when he heard his own name called. "Hugh! Come here!"

Reluctantly he left his discovery, and sought out the twins. "Come see what I've found," he began.

"Never mind," Joe cut him short. "Look at that."

Hugh looked. "That" was a Converter. Quite small, but indubitably a Converter. "It doesn't make sense," Jim protested. "An apartment this size doesn't need a Converter. That thing would supply power and light for half the Ship. What do you make of it, Hugh?"

Hugh examined it. "I don't know," he admitted, "but if you think this is strange, come see what I've found."

"What have you found?"

"Come see."

The twins followed him, and saw a small compartment, one wall of which appeared to be of glass—black, as if the far side were obscured. Facing the wall were two acceleration chairs, side by side. The arms and the lap desks of the chairs were covered with patterns of little shining lights of the same sort as the control lights on the chairs in the Main Control Room.

Joe-Jim made no comment at first, save for a low whistle from Jim. He sat down in one of the chairs and started experimenting cautiously with the controls. Hugh sat down beside him. Joe-Jim covered a group of white lights on the right-hand arm of his chair; the lights in the apartment went out. When he lifted his hand the tiny control lights were blue instead of white. Neither Joe-Jim nor Hugh was startled when the lights went out; they had expected it, for the control involved corresponded to similar controls in the Control Room.

Joe-Jim fumbled around, trying to find controls which would produce a simulacrum of the heavens on the blank glass before him. There were no such controls and he had no way of knowing that the glass was an actual view port, obscured by the hull of the Ship proper, rather than a view screen.

But he did manage to actuate the controls that occupied the corresponding position. These controls were labeled LAUNCHING; Joe-Jim had disregarded the label because he did not understand it. Actuating them produced no very remarkable results, except that a red light blinked rapidly and a transparency below the label came into life. It read: AIR-LOCK OPEN.

Which was very lucky for Joe-Jim, Hugh, and Bobo. Had they closed the doors behind them and had the little

Converter contained even a few grams of mass available for power, they would have found themselves launched suddenly into space, in a Ship's boat unequipped for a trip and whose controls they understood only by analogy with those in the Control Room. Perhaps they could have maneuvered the boat back into its cradle; more likely they would have crashed attempting it.

But Hugh and Joe-Jim were not yet aware that the "apartment" they had entered was a spacecraft; the idea of a Ship's boat was still foreign to them.

"Turn on the lights," Hugh requested. Joe-Jim did so.

"Well?" Hugh went on. "What do you make of it?"

"It seems pretty obvious," answered Jim. "This is another Control Room. We didn't guess it was here because we couldn't open the door."

"That doesn't make sense," Joe objected. "Why should there be two Control Rooms for one Ship?"

"Why should a man have two heads?" his brother reasoned. "From my point of view, you are obviously a supernumerary."

"It's not the same thing; we were born that way. But this didn't just happen—the Ship was *built*."

"So what?" Jim argued. "We carry two knives, don't we? And we weren't born with 'em. It's a good idea to have a spare."

"But you can't control the Ship from here," Joe protested. "You can't *see* anything from here. If you wanted a second set of controls, the place to put them would be the Captain's veranda, where you can see the stars."

"How about that?" Jim asked, indicating the wall of glass.

"Use your head," his brother advised. "It faces the wrong direction. It looks into the Ship, not out. And it's not an arrangement like the Control Room; there isn't any way to mirror the stars on it."

"Maybe we haven't located the controls for it."

"Even *so*, you've forgotten something. How about that little Converter?"

"What about it?"

"It must have some significance. It's not here by accident. I'll bet you that these controls have something to do with that Converter."

"Why?"

"Why not? Why are they here together if there isn't some connection?"

Hugh broke his puzzled silence. Everything the twins had said seemed to make sense, even the contradictions. It was all very confusing. But the Converter, the little Converter—"Say, look," he burst out.

"Look at what?"

"Do you suppose—Do you think that maybe this part of the Ship could *move?*"

"Naturally. The whole Ship moves."

"No," said Hugh, "no, no. I don't mean that at all. Suppose it moved by *itself*. These controls and the little Converter—suppose it could *move* right away from the Ship."

"That's pretty fantastic."

"Maybe so—but if it's true, *this is the way out.*"

"Huh?" said Joe. "Nonsense. No door to the Outside here either."

"But there would be if this apartment were moved away from the Ship—the way we came in!"

The two heads snapped simultaneously toward him as if jerked by the same string. Then they looked at each other and fell to arguing. Joe-Jim repeated his experiment with the controls. "See?" Joe pointed out. "'Launching.' It means to start something, to push something away."

"Then why doesn't it?"

"'Air-Lock Open.' The doors we came through—it has to be that. Everything else is closed."

"Let's try it."

"We would have to start the Converter first."

"O.K."

"Not so fast. Get out, and maybe you can't come back. We'd starve."

"Hm-m-m—we'll wait a while."

Hugh listened to the discussion while snooping around the control panels, trying to figure them out. There was a stowage space under the lap desk of his chair; he fished into it, encountered something, and hauled it out. "See what I've found!"

"What is it?" asked Joe. "Oh—a book. Lot of them back in the room next to the Converter." "Let's see it," said Jim.

But Hugh had opened it himself. " 'Log, Starship *Van-guard,* '" he spelled out, " '2 June, 2172. Cruising as before—' "

"What!" yelled Joe. "Let me see that!"

" '3 June. Cruising as before. 4 June. Cruising as before. Captain's mast for rewards and punishments held at 1300. See Administration Log. 5 June. Cruising as before—' "

"Gimme that!"

"Wait!" said Hugh. " '6 June. Mutiny broke out at 0431. The watch became aware of it by visiplate. Huff, Metal-smith Ordinary, screened the control station and called on the watch to surrender, designating himself as "Captain." The officer of the watch ordered him to consider himself under arrest and signaled the Captain's cabin. No answer.

" '0435. Communications failed. The officer of the watch dispatched a party of three to notify the Captain, turn out the chief proctor, and assist in the arrest of Huff.

" '0441. Converter power off; free flight.

" '0502. Lacy, Crewman Ordinary, messenger-of-the-watch, one of the party of three sent below, returned to the control station alone. He reported verbally that the other two, Malcolm Young and Arthur Sears, were dead and that he had been permitted to return in order to notify the watch to surrender. The mutineers gave 0515 as a deadline.' "

The next entry was in a different hand: " '0545. I have made every attempt to get into communication with other stations and officers in the Ship, without success. I conceive it as my duty, under the circumstances, to leave the control station without being properly relieved, and attempt to restore order down below. My decision may be faulty, since we are unarmed, but I see no other course open to me.

" 'Jean Baldwin, Pilot Officer Third Class, Officer of the Watch.' "

"Is that all?" demanded Joe.

"No," said Hugh. " '1 October (approximately), 2172. I, Theodor Mawson, formerly Storekeeper Ordinary, have been selected this date as Captain of the *Vanguard.* Since the last entry in this log there have been enormous changes. The mutiny has been suppressed, or more properly, has died out, but with tragic cost. Every pilot officer, every engineering officer, is dead, or believed to be dead. I would not have been chosen Captain had there been a qualified man left.

"'Approximately ninety per cent of the personnel are dead. Not all of that number died in the original outbreak; no crops have been planted since the mutiny; our food-stocks are low. There seems to be clear evidence of cannibalism among the mutineers who have not surrendered.

"'My immediate task must be to restore some semblance of order and discipline among the Crew. Crops must be planted. A regular watch must be instituted at the auxiliary Converter on which we are dependent for heat and light and power.'"

The next entry was undated. "'I have been far too busy to keep this log up properly. Truthfully, I do not know the date even approximately. The Ship's clocks no longer run. That may be attributable to the erratic operation of the auxiliary Converter, or it may possibly be an effect of radiations from outer space. We no longer have an anti-radiation shield around the Ship, since the Main Converter is not in operation. My Chief Engineer assures me that the Main Converter could be started, but we have no one fitted to astrogate. I have tried to teach myself astrogation from the books at hand, but the mathematics involved are very difficult.

"'About one newborn child out of twenty is deformed. I have instituted a Spartan code—such children are not permitted to live. It is harsh, but necessary.

"'I am growing very old and feeble and must consider the selection of my successor. I am the last member of the crew to be born on Earth, and even I have little recollection of it—I was five when my parents embarked. I do not know my own age, but certain unmistakable signs tell me that the time is not far away when I, too, must make the Trip to the Converter.

"'There has been a curious change in orientation in my people. Never having lived on a planet, it becomes more difficult as time passes for them to comprehend anything not connected with the Ship. I have ceased trying to talk to them about it—it is hardly a kindness anyhow, as I have no hope of leading them out of the darkness. Theirs is a hard life at best; they raise a crop only to have it raided by the outlaws who still flourish on the upper levels. Why speak to them of better things?

" 'Rather than pass this on to my successor I have decided to attempt to hide it, if possible, in the single Ship's boat left by the mutineers who escaped. It will be safe there a long time—otherwise some witless fool may decide to use it for fuel for the Converter. I caught the man on watch feeding it with the last of a set of *Encyclopaedia Terrestriana*—priceless books. The idiot had never been taught to read! Some rule must be instituted concerning books.

" 'This is my last entry. I have put off making the attempt to place this log in safekeeping, because it is very perilous to ascend above the lower decks. But my life is no longer valuable; I wish to die knowing that a true record is left.

" 'Theodor Mawson, Captain.' "

Even the twins were silent for a long time after Hugh stopped reading. At last Joe heaved a long sigh and said, "So that's how it happened."

"The poor guy," Hugh said softly.

"Who? Captain Mawson? Why so?"

"No, not Captain Mawson. That other guy, Pilot Officer Baldwin. Think of him going out through that door, with *Huff* on the other side." Hugh shivered. In spite of his enlightenment, he subconsciously envisioned Huff, "Huff the Accursed, first to sin," as about twice as high as Joe-Jim, twice as strong as Bobo, and having fangs rather than teeth.

Hugh borrowed a couple of porters from Ertz—porters whom Ertz was using to fetch the pickled bodies of the war casualties to the Main Converter for fuel—and used them to provision the Ship's boat; water, breadstuffs, preserved meats, mass for the Converter. He did not report the matter to Narby, nor did he report the discovery of the boat itself. He had no conscious reason—Narby irritated him.

The star of their destination grew and grew, swelled until it showed a visible disc and was too bright to be stared at long. Its bearing changed rapidly, for a star; it pulled across the backdrop of the stellarium dome. Left uncontrolled, the Ship would have swung part way around it in a broad hyperbola and receded again into the depths of the darkness. It took Hugh the equivalent of many weeks to calculate the elements of the trajectory; it took still longer for Ertz and Joe-Jim to check his figures and satisfy themselves that the preposterous answers were right. It took even longer to convince Ertz that the way to rendezvous in space was to apply a force that pushed one *away* from where one wished to go—that is to say, dig in the heels, put on the brakes, kill the momentum.

In fact it took a series of experiments in free flight on the level of weightlessness to sell him the idea—otherwise he would have favored finishing the Trip by the simple expedient of crashing headlong into the star at top speed. Thereafter Hugh and Joe-Jim calculated how to apply acceleration to kill the speed of the *Vanguard* and warp her into an eccentric ellipse around the star. After that they would search for planets.

Ertz had a little trouble understanding the difference between a planet and a star. Alan never did get it.

"If my numbering is correct," Hugh informed Ertz "we should start accelerating any time now."

"O.K.," Ertz told him. "Main Drive is ready—over two hundred bodies and a lot of waste mass. What are we waiting for?"

"Let's see Narby and get permission to start."

"Why ask him?"

Hugh shrugged. "He's Captain. He'll want to know."

"All right. Let's pick up Joe-Jim and get on with it." They left Hugh's apartment and went to Joe-Jim's. Joe-Jim was not there, but they found Alan looking for him, too.

"Squatty says he's gone down to the Captain's office," Alan informed him.

"So? It's just as well—we'll see him there. Alan, old boy, you know what?"

"What?"

"The time has arrived. We're going to do it! Start moving the Ship!"

Alan looked round-eyed. "Gee! Right now?"

"Just as soon as we can notify the Captain. Come along, if you like."

"You bet! Wait while I tell my woman." He darted away to his own quarters nearby.

"He pampers that wench," remarked Ertz.

"Sometimes you can't help it," said Hugh with a faraway look.

Alan returned promptly, although it was evident that he had taken time to change to a fresh breechcloth. "O.K.," he bubbled. "Let's go!"

Alan approached the Captain's office with a proud step. He was an important guy now, he exulted to himself—he'd march on through with his friends while the guards saluted —no more of this business of being pushed around.

But the doorkeeper did not stand aside, although he did salute—while placing himself so that he filled the door. "Gangway, man!" Ertz said gruffly.

"Yes, sir," acknowledged the guard, without moving. "Your weapons, please."

"What! Don't you know me, you idiot? I'm the Chief Engineer."

"Yes, sir. Leave your weapons with me, please. Regulations."

Ertz put a hand on the man's shoulder and shoved. The guard stood firm. "I'm sorry, sir. No one approaches the Captain wearing weapons. No one."

"Well, I'll be damned!"

"He remembers what happened to the old Captain," Hugh observed *sotto voce*. "He's smart." He drew his own knife and tossed it to the guard. who caught it neatly by the hilt. Ertz looked, shrugged, and handed over his own. Alan, considerably crestfallen, passed his own pair over with a look that should have shortened the guard's life.

Narby was talking; Joe-Jim was scowling on both his faces; Bobo looked puzzled, and naked, unfinished, without his ubiquitous knives and slingshot. "The matter is closed, Joe-Jim. That is my decision. I've granted you the favor of explaining my reasons, but it does not matter whether you like them or not."

"What's the trouble?" inquired Hugh.

Narby looked up. "Oh—I'm glad you came in. Your mutie friend seems to be in doubt as to who is Captain."

"What's up?"

"He," growled Jim, hooking a thumb toward Narby, "seems to think he's going to disarm all the muties."

"Well, the war's over, isn't it?"

"It wasn't agreed on. The muties were to become part of the Crew. Take the knives away from the muties and the Crew will kill them off in no time. It's not fair. The Crew have knives."

"The time will come when they won't," Narby predicted, "but I'll do it at my own time in my own way. This is the first step. What did you want to see me about, Ertz?"

"Ask Hugh." Narby turned to Hugh.

"I've come to notify you, Captain Narby," Hugh stated formally, "that we are about to start the Main Converter and move the Ship."

Narby looked surprised but not disconcerted. "I'm afraid you will have to postpone that. I am not yet ready to permit officers to go up to no-weight."

"It won't be necessary," Hugh explained. "Ertz and I can handle the first maneuvers alone. But we can't wait. If the Ship is not moved at once, the Trip won't be finished in your lifetime nor mine."

"Then it must," Narby replied evenly, "wait."

"What?" cried Hugh. "Narby, don't you *want* to finish the Trip?"

"I'm in no hurry."

"What sort of damn foolishness is this?" Ertz demanded. "What's got into you, Fin? Of course we move the Ship."

Narby drummed on his desk top before replying. Then he said, "Since there seems to be some slight misunderstanding as to who gives orders around here, I might as well let you have it straight. Hoyland, as long as your pastimes did not interfere with the administration of the Ship, I was willing for you to amuse yourself. I granted that willingly, for you have been very useful in your own way. But when your crazy beliefs become a possible source of corruption to good morals and a danger to the peace and security of the Ship, I have to crack down."

Hugh had opened and closed his mouth several times during this speech. Finally he managed to get out: "Crazy? Did you say crazy?"

"Yes, I did. For a man to believe that the solid Ship can move means that he is either crazy, or an ignorant religious fanatic. Since both of you have the advantage of a scientist's training, I assume that you have lost your minds."

"Good Jordan!" said Hugh. "The man has seen with his own eyes, he's seen the immortal stars—yet he sits there and calls *us* crazy!"

"What's the meaning of this, Narby?" Ertz inquired coldly. "Why the razzle-dazzle? You aren't kidding anyone—you've been to the Control Room, you've been to the Captain's veranda, you *know* the Ship moves."

"You interest me, Ertz," commented Narby, looking him over. "I've wondered whether you were playing up to Hoyland's delusions, or were deluded yourself. Now I see that you are crazy too."

Ertz kept his temper. "Explain yourself. You've seen the Control Room; how can you contend that the Ship does not move?"

Narby smiled. "I thought you were a better engineer than you appear to be, Ertz. The Control Room is an enormous hoax. You know yourself that those lights are turned on and off by switches—a very clever piece of engineering. My theory is that it was used to strike awe in the minds of the superstitious and make them believe in the ancient myths. But we don't need it any more, the Crew believe without it. It's a source of distraction now —I'm going to have it destroyed and the door sealed up."

Hugh went all to pieces at this, sputtered incoherently, and would have grappled with Narby had not Ertz restrained him. "Easy, Hugh," he admonished. Joe-Jim took Hugh by the arm, his own faces stony masks.

Ertz went on quietly, "Suppose what you say is true. Suppose that the Main Converter and the Main Drive itself are nothing but dummies and that we can never start them, what about the Captain's veranda? You've *seen* the stars there, not just an engineered shadow show."

Narby laughed. "Ertz, you are stupider than I ever guessed. I admit that the display in the veranda had me mystified at first—not that I ever believed in it! But the Control Room gave the clue—it's an illusion, a piece of skillful engineering. Behind that glass is another compartment, about the same size and unlighted. Against that darkness those tiny moving lights give the effect of a bottomless hole. It's essentially the same trick as the one used in the Control Room.

"It's obvious," he went on. "I'm surprised that you did not see it. When an apparent fact runs contrary to logic and common sense, it's obvious that you have failed to interpret the fact correctly. The most obvious fact of nature is the reality of the Ship itself, solid, immutable, complete. Any so-called fact which appears to dispute that is bound to be an illusion. Knowing that, I looked for the trick behind the illusion and found it."

"Wait," said Ertz. "Do you mean that you have been on the other side of the glass in the Captain's veranda and seen these trick lights you talk about?"

"No," admitted Narby, "it wasn't necessary. No doubt it would be easy enough to do so, but it isn't necessary. I don't have to cut myself to know that knives are sharp."

"So—" Ertz paused and thought a moment. "I'll make a deal with you. If Hugh and I are crazy in our beliefs, no harm is done as long as we keep our mouths shut. We'll try to move the Ship. If we fail we're wrong and you're right."

"The Captain does not bargain," Narby pointed out. "However—I'll consider it. That's all. You may go."

Ertz turned to go, unsatisfied but checked for the moment. He caught sight of Joe-Jim's faces, and turned back. "One more thing," he said. "What's this about the muties? Why are you shoving Joe-Jim around? He and his boys made you Captain—you've got to be fair about this."

Narby's smiling superiority cracked for a moment.

"Don't interfere, Ertz! Groups of armed savages can't be tolerated. That's final."

"You can do what you like with the prisoners," Jim stated, "but my own gang keep their knives. They were promised good eating forever if they fought for you. They keep their knives. And that's final!"

Narby looked him up and down. "Joe-Jim," he remarked, "I have long believed that the only good mutie was a dead mutie. You do much to confirm my opinion. It will interest you to know that, by this time, your gang *is* disarmed—and dead in the bargain. That's why I sent for you!"

The guards piled in, whether by signal or previous arrangement it was impossible to say. Caught flatfooted, naked, weaponless, the five found themselves each with an armed man at his back before they could rally. "Take them away," ordered Narby.

Bobo whined and looked to Joe-Jim for guidance. Joe caught his eye. "Up, Bobo!"

The dwarf jumped straight for Joe-Jim's captor, careless of the knife at his back. Forced to split his attention, the man lost a vital half second. Joe-Jim kicked him in the stomach, and appropriated his blade.

Hugh was on the deck, deadlocked with his man, his fist clutched around the knife wrist. Joe-Jim thrust and the struggle ceased. The two-headed man looked around, saw a mixed pile-up of four bodies, Ertz, Alan, two others. Joe-Jim used his knife judiciously, being careful to match the faces with the bodies. Presently his friends emerged. "Get their knives," he ordered superfluously.

His words were drowned by a high, agonized scream. Bobo, still without a knife, had resorted to his primal weapons. His late captor's face was a bloody mess, half bitten away.

"Get his knife," said Joe.

"Can't reach it," Bobo admitted guiltily. The reason was evident—the hilt protruded from Bobo's ribs, just below his right shoulder blade.

Joe-Jim examined it, touched it gently. It was stuck. "Can you walk?"

"Sure," grunted Bobo, and grimaced.

"Let it stay where it is. Alan! With me. Hugh and Bill—cover rear. Bobo in the middle."

"Where's Narby?" demanded Ertz, dabbing at a wound on his cheekbone.

But Narby was gone—ducked out through the rear door behind his desk. And it was locked.

Clerks scattered before them in the outer office; Joe-Jim knifed the guard at the outer door while he was still raising his whistle. Hastily they retrieved their own weapons and added them to those they had seized. They fled upward.

Two decks above inhabited levels Bobo stumbled and fell. Joe-Jim picked him up. "Can you make it?"

The dwarf nodded dumbly, blood on his lips. They climbed. Twenty decks or so higher it became evident that Bobo could no longer climb, though they had taken turns in boosting him from the rear. But weight was lessened appreciably at that level; Alan braced himself and picked up the solid form as if it were a child. They climbed.

Joe-Jim relieved Alan. They climbed.

Ertz relieved Joe-Jim. Hugh relieved Ertz.

They reached the level on which they lived forward of their group apartments. Hugh turned in that direction. "Put him down," commanded Joe. "Where do you think you are going?"

Hugh settled the wounded man to the deck. "Home. Where else?"

"Fool! That's where they will look for us first."

"Where *do* we go?"

"Nowhere—in the Ship. We go out of the Ship!"

"Huh?"

"The Ship's boat."

"He's right," agreed Ertz. "The whole Ship's against us now."

"But . . . but—" Hugh surrendered. "It's a long chance—but we'll try it." He started again in the direction of their homes.

"Hey!" shouted Jim. "Not that way."

"We have to get our women."

"To Huff with the women! You'll get caught. There's no time." But Ertz and Alan started off without question. "Oh—all right!" Jim snorted. "But hurry! I'll stay with Bobo."

Joe-Jim sat down, took the dwarf's head in his lap, and

made a careful examination. His skin was gray and damp; a long red stain ran down from his right shoulder. Bobo sighed bubblingly and rubbed his head against Joe-Jim's thigh. "Bobo tired, Boss."

Joe-Jim patted his head. "Easy," said Jim, "this is going to hurt." Lifting the wounded man slightly, he cautiously worked the blade loose and withdrew it from the wound. Blood poured out freely.

Joe-Jim examined the knife, noted the deadly length of steel, and measured it against the wound. "He'll never make it," whispered Joe.

Jim caught his eye. "Well?"

Joe nodded slowly. Joe-Jim tried the blade he had just extracted from the wound against his own thigh, and discarded it in favor of one of his own razor-edged tools. He took the dwarf's chin in his left hand and Joe commanded, "Look at me, Bobo!"

Bobo looked up, answered inaudibly. Joe held his eye. "Good Bobo! Strong Bobo!" The dwarf grinned as if he heard and understood, but made no attempt to reply. His master pulled his head a little to one side; the blade bit deep, snicking the jugular vein without touching the windpipe. "Good Bobo!" Joe repeated. Bobo grinned again.

When the eyes were glassy and breathing had unquestionably stopped, Joe-Jim stood up, letting the head and shoulders roll from him. He shoved the body with his foot to the side of the passage, and stared down the direction in which the others had gone. They should be back by now.

He stuck the salvaged blade in his belt and made sure that all his weapons were loose and ready.

They arrived on a dead run. "A little trouble," Hugh explained breathlessly. "Squatty's dead. No more of your men around. Dead maybe—Narby probably meant it. Here—" He handed him a long knife and the body armor that had been built for Joe-Jim, with its great wide cage of steel, fit to cover two heads.

Ertz and Alan wore armor, as did Hugh. The women did not—none had been built for them. Joe-Jim noted that Hugh's younger wife bore a fresh swelling on her lip, as if someone had persuaded her with a heavy hand. Her eyes were stormy though her manner was docile. The older wife, Chloe, seemed to take the events in her stride. Ertz's was crying softly; Alan's wench reflected the bewilderment of her master.

"How's Bobo?" Hugh inquired, as he settled Joe-Jim's armor in place.

"Made the Trip," Joe informed him.

"So? Well, that's that—let's go."

They stopped short of the level of no-weight and worked forward, because the women were not adept at weightless flying. When they reached the bulkhead which separated the Control Room and boat pockets from the body of the Ship, they went up. There was neither alarm nor ambush, although Joe thought that he saw a head show as they reached one deck. He mentioned it to his brother but not to the others.

The door to the boat pocket stuck and Bobo was not there to free it. The men tried it in succession, sweating with the strain. Joe-Jim tried it a second time, Joe relaxing and letting Jim control their muscles, that they might not fight each other. The door gave. "Get 'em inside!" snapped Jim.

"And fast!" Joe confirmed. "They're on us." He had kept lookout while his brother strove. A shout from down the line reinforced his warning.

The twins faced around to meet the threat while the men shoved the women in. Alan's fuzzy-headed mate chose that moment to go to pieces, squalled, and tried to run, but weightlessness defeated her. Hugh nabbed her, headed her inside and booted her heartily with his foot.

Joe-Jim let a blade go at long throwing range to slow down the advance. It accomplished its purpose; his opponents, half a dozen of them, checked their advance. Then, apparently on signal, six knives cut the air simultaneously.

Jim felt something strike him, felt no pain, and concluded that the armor had saved him. "Missed us, Joe," he exulted.

There was no answer. Jim turned his head, tried to look

at his brother. A few inches from his eye a knife stuck through the bars of the helmet; its point was buried deep in Joe's left eye.

His brother was dead.

Hugh stuck his head back out of the door. "Come on, Joe-Jim," he shouted. "We're all in."

"Get inside," ordered Jim. "Close the door."

"But—"

"Get inside!" Jim turned, and shoved him in the face, closing the door as he did so. Hugh had one startled glimpse of the knife and sagging, lifeless face it pinned. Then the door closed against him, and he heard the lever turn.

Jim turned back at the attackers. Shoving himself away from the bulkhead with legs which were curiously heavy, he plunged toward them, his great armlong knife, more a bolo than a sword, grasped with both hands. Knives sang toward him, clattered against his breastplate, bit into his legs. He swung—a wide awkward two-handed stroke which gutted an opponent—nearly cut him in two. "That's for Joe!"

The blow stopped him. He turned in the air, steadied himself, and swung again. "That's for Bobo!"

They closed on him; he swung widely, caring not where he hit as long as his blade met resistance. "And that's for me!"

A knife planted itself in his thigh. It did not even slow him up; legs were dispensable in no-weight. "'One for all!'"

A man was on his back now—he could feel him. No matter—here was one before him, too—one who could feel steel. As he swung, he shouted, "All for o—" The words trailed off, but the stroke was finished.

Hugh tried to open the door which had been slammed in his face. He was unable to do so—if there were means provided to do so, he was unable to figure them out. He pressed an ear against the steel and listened, but the airtight door gave back no clue.

Ertz touched him on the shoulder. "Come on," he said. "Where's Joe-Jim?"

"He stayed behind."

"What! Open the door—get him."

"I can't, it won't open. He meant to stay, he closed it himself."

"But we've got to get him—we're blood-sworn."

"I think," said Hugh, with a sudden flash of insight, "that's why he stayed behind." He told Ertz what he had seen.

"Anyhow," he concluded, "it's the *End of the Trip* to him. Get on back and feed mass to that Converter. I want power." They entered the Ship's boat proper; Hugh closed the air-lock doors behind them. "Alan!" he called out. "We're going to start. Keep those damned women out of the way."

He settled himself in the pilot's chair, and cut the lights.

In the darkness he covered a pattern of green lights. A transparency flashed on the lap desk: DRIVE READY. Ertz was on the job. Here goes! he thought, and actuated the launching combination. There was a short pause, a short and sickening lurch—*a twist*. It frightened him, since he had no way of knowing that the launching tracks were pitched to offset the normal spinning of the Ship.

The glass of the view port before him was speckled with stars; they were free—moving!

But the spread of jeweled lights was not unbroken, as it invariably had been when seen from the veranda, or seen mirrored on the Control Room walls; a great, gross, ungainly shape gleamed softly under the light of the star whose system they had entered. At first he could not account for it. Then with a rush of superstitious awe he realized that he was looking at the Ship itself, the true Ship, seen from the Outside. In spite of his long intellectual awareness of the true nature of the Ship, he had never visualized looking at it. The stars, yes—the surface of a planet, he had struggled with that concept—but the outer surface of the Ship, no.

When he did see it, it shocked him.

Alan touched him. "Hugh, what is it?"

Hoyland tried to explain to him. Alan shook his head, and blinked his eyes. "I don't get it."

"Never mind. Bring Ertz up here. Fetch the women, too—we'll let them see it."

"All right. But," he added, with sound intuition, "it's a mistake to show the women. You'll scare 'em silly—they ain't even seen the stars."

Luck, sound engineering design, and a little knowledge. Good design, ten times that much luck, and a precious little knowledge. It was luck that had placed the Ship near a star with a planetary system, luck that the Ship arrived there with a speed low enough for Hugh to counteract it in a ship's auxiliary craft, luck that he learned to handle it after a fashion before they starved or lost themselves in deep space.

It was good design that provided the little craft with a great reserve of power and speed. The designers had anticipated that the pioneers might need to explore the far-flung planets of a solar system; they had provided for it in the planning of the Ship's boats, with a large factor of safety. Hugh strained that factor to the limit.

It was luck that placed them near the plane of planetary motion, luck that, when Hugh did manage to gun the tiny projectile into a closed orbit, the orbit agreed in direction with the rotation of the planets.

Luck that the eccentric ellipse he achieved should cause them to crawl up on a giant planet so that he was eventually able to identify it as such by sight.

For otherwise they might have spun around that star until they all died of old age, ignoring for the moment the readier hazards of hunger and thirst, without ever coming close enough to a planet to pick it out from the stars.

There is a misconception, geocentric and anthropomorphic, common to the large majority of the earthbound, which causes them to visualize a planetary system stereoscopically. The mind's eye sees a sun, remote from a backdrop of stars, and surrounded by spinning apples—the planets. Step out on your balcony and look. Can you tell the planets from the stars? Venus you may pick out with ease, but could you tell it from Canopus, if you had not previously been introduced? That little red speck—is it Mars, or is it Antares? How would you know, if you were as ignorant as Hugh Hoyland? Blast for Antares, believing it to be a planet, and you will never live to have grandchildren.

The great planet that they crawled up on, till it showed a visible naked-eye disc, was larger than Jupiter, a fit companion to the star, somewhat younger and larger than the Sun, around which it swung at a lordly distance. Hugh blasted back, killing his speed over many sleeps, to bring the Ship into a path around the planet. The maneuver brought him close enough to see its moons.

Luck helped him again. He had planned to ground on the great planet, knowing no better. Had he been able to do so they would have lived just long enough to open the air-lock.

But he was short of mass, after the titanic task of pulling them out of the headlong hyperbolic plunge around and past the star and warping them into a closed orbit about the star, then into a subordinate orbit around the great planet. He pored over the ancient books, substituted endlessly in the equations the ancients had set down as the laws for moving bodies, figured and refigured, and tried even the calm patience of Chloe.

The other wife, the unnamed one, kept out of his sight after losing a tooth, quite suddenly.

But he got no answer that did not require him to use some, at least, of the precious, irreplaceable ancient books for fuel. Yes, even though they stripped themselves naked and chucked in their knives, the mass of the books would still be needed.

He would have preferred to dispense with one of his wives. He decided to ground on one of the moons.

Luck again. Coincidence of such colossal proportions that one need not be expected to believe it—for the moon-planet was suitable for human terrestrial life. Never mind—skip over it rapidly; the combination of circumstances is of the same order needed to produce such a planet in the first place. Our own planet, under our feet, is of the "There ain't no such animal!" variety. It is a ridiculous improbability.

Hugh's luck was a ridiculous improbability.

Good design handled the next phase. Although he had learned to maneuver the little Ship out in space where there is elbow room, landing is another and a ticklish matter.

He would have crashed any spacecraft designed before the designing of the *Vanguard*. But the designers of the *Vanguard* had known that the Ship's auxiliary craft would be piloted and grounded by at least the second generation of explorers; green pilots must make those landings unassisted. They planned for it.

Hugh got the vessel down into the stratosphere and straightened it triumphantly into a course that would with certainty kill them all.

The autopilots took over.

Hugh stormed and swore, producing some words which diverted Alan's attention and admiration from the view out of the port. But nothing he could do would cause the craft to respond. It settled in its own way and leveled off at a thousand feet, an altitude which it maintained regardless of changing contour.

"Hugh, the stars are gone!"

"I know it."

"But Jordan! Hugh—what happened to them?"

Hugh glared at Alan. "I—don't—know—and—I—don't care! You get aft with the women and stop asking silly questions."

Alan departed reluctantly with a backward look at the surface of the planet and the bright sky. It interested him, but he did not marvel much at it—his ability to marvel had been overstrained.

It was some hours before Hugh discovered that a hitherto ignored group of control lights set in motion a chain of events whereby the autopilot would ground the Ship. Since he found this out experimentally he did not exactly choose the place of landing. But the unwinking stereo-eyes of the autopilot fed its data to the "brain"; the submolar mechanism selected and rejected; the Ship grounded gently on a rolling high prairie near a clump of trees.

Ertz came forward. "What's happened, Hugh?"

Hugh waved at the view port. "We're there." He was too tired to make much of it, too tired and too emotionally exhausted. His weeks of fighting a fight he understood but poorly, hunger, and lately thirst—years of feeding on a consuming ambition, these left him with little ability to enjoy his goal when it arrived.

But they had landed, they had finished Jordan's Trip. He was not unhappy; at peace rather, and very tired.

Ertz stared out. "Jordan!" he muttered. Then, "Let's go out."

"All right."

Alan came forward, as they were opening the air-lock, and the women pressed after him. "Are we there, Captain?"

"Shut up," said Hugh.

The women crowded up to the deserted view port; Alan explained to them, importantly and incorrectly, the scene outside. Ertz got the last door open.

They sniffed at the air. "It's *cold*," said Ertz. In fact the temperature was perhaps five degrees less than the steady monotony of the Ship's temperature, but Ertz was experiencing weather for the first time.

"Nonsense," said Hugh, faintly annoyed that any fault should be found with "his" planet. "It's just your imagination."

"Maybe," Ertz conceded. He paused uneasily. "Going out?" he added.

"Of course." Mastering his own reluctance, Hugh pushed him aside and dropped five feet to the ground "Come on—it's fine."

Ertz joined him, and stood close to him. Both of them remained close to the Ship. "It's big, isn't it?" Ertz said in a hushed voice.

"Well, we knew it would be," Hugh snapped, annoyed with himself for having the same lost feeling.

"Hi!" Alan peered cautiously out of the door. "Can I come down? Is it all right?"

"Come ahead."

Alan eased himself gingerly over the edge and joined them. He looked around and whistled. "Gosh!"

Their first sortie took them all of fifty feet from the Ship.

They huddled close together for silent comfort, and watched their feet to keep from stumbling on this strange

uneven deck. They made it without incident until Alan
looked up from the ground and found himself for the first
time in his life with nothing *close* to him. He was hit by
vertigo and acute agoraphobia; he moaned, closed his
eyes and fell.

"What in the Ship?" demanded Ertz, looking around.
Then it hit him.

Hugh fought against it. It pulled him to his knees, but
he fought it, steadying himself with one hand on the
ground. However, he had the advantage of having stared
out through the view port for endless time—neither Alan
nor Ertz were cowards.

"Alan!" his wife shrilled from the open door. "Alan!
Come back here!" Alan opened one eye, managed to get
it focused on the Ship, and started inching back on
his belly.

"Alan!" commanded Hugh. "Stop that! Sit up."

Alan did so, with the air of a man pushed too far. "Open
your eyes!" Alan obeyed cautiously, reclosed them hastily.

"Just sit still and you'll be all right," Hugh added. "I'm
all right already." To prove it he stood up. He was still
dizzy, but he made it. Ertz sat up.

The sun had crossed a sizable piece of the sky, enough
time had passed for a well-fed man to become hungry—and
they were not well fed. Even the women were outside—that
had been accomplished by the simple expedient of going
back in and pushing them out. They had not ventured away
from the side of the Ship, but sat huddled against it. But
their menfolk had even learned to walk singly, even in
open spaces. Alan thought nothing of strutting a full fifty
yards away from the shadow of the Ship, and did so more
than once, in full sight of the women.

It was on one such journey that a small animal native
to the planet let his curiosity exceed his caution. Alan's
knife knocked him over and left him kicking. Alan scurried
to the spot, grabbed his fat prize by one leg, and bore it
proudly back to Hugh. "Look, Hugh, look! Good eating!"

Hugh looked with approval. His first strange fright of

the place had passed and had been replaced with a warm deep feeling, a feeling that he had come at last to his long home. This seemed a good omen.

"Yes," he agreed. "Good eating. From now on, Alan, always Good Eating."